PRAISE FOR *WATERMARK*

"If you have faith in Flannery O'Connor's fiction, or if you watch Werner Herzog's films with a sense of awe, then Christy Ann Conlin's collection of stories is for you. Equal parts lovely and loathsome, terrifying and tender, this elemental book works with the rawest of raw materials. If you have a family, or if you live in this world, I bet you'll see yourself reflected in Conlin's carefully polished carnival mirror. This is honest and revealing writing from an artist at the top of her craft." —Alexander MacLeod, author of *Light Lifting*

"*Watermark* is propulsive. These linked stories are Gothic dark and sparking with brilliant twists. Characters so vivid you can hear their voices, feel their pulse. Here are deep psychological fractures and betrayals, loss and long-ing. Adventure and abandon. Conlin's characters are splendidly complex; they are sometimes prisoners, and sometimes breaking free. This book is a dangerous joyride." —Lisa Moore, author of *Caught* and *Something for Everyone*

"These stories achieve a dizzying balance of light and dark—the magical with the murderous. Over and over again, Conlin masterfully depicts the lush, somehow uncanny splendour of high summer only to chill us with a counterbalancing night world of hidden creatures and terrible human secrets. The results make for mesmerizing reading." —Lynn Coady, author of *Hellgoing* and *Watching You Without Me*

"Conlin's characters are fierce, lonely, dangerous, and wild. This is the best short story collection I've read in years." —Annabel Lyon, author of *Oxygen* and *The Golden Mean*

"From the Gothic heart of the Annapolis Valley to the dreamlike shores of British Columbia, these stories sparkle with wickedness and dark beauty, reminding us again that Conlin is one of Canada's most daring and original writers. The range and breadth of style and voice in this collection is astonishing, and her gift for the uncanny is as assured as her masterful writing. Whether it's through the skewed vision of a heartbroken widower or the vivid delusions of an unrepentant killer, she presents a moving and uncompromising exploration of the deep undercurrents of the human psyche, and the tricks that our minds play—on ourselves and each other." —Kerry Lee Powell, author of *Willem de Kooning's Paintbrush*

"*Watermark* takes us beyond mere appearances, offering intimate portraits of characters you quickly realize you only think you know. These are powerful stories that tell secrets—that are interested in, and unafraid of, all the messy details that make up a person, a life." —Johanna Skibsrud, author of *The Sentimentalists* and *Quartet for the End of Time*

"Conlin's prose is both gorgeous and unsettling, her characters both enigmatic and startlingly familiar. Her stories reveal the beauty in the darkness, and the humanity in the inhumane. *Watermark* is a rare gem of a book that will leave you breathless." —Amy Jones, author of *We're All in This Together* and *Every Little Piece of Me*

Also by Christy Ann Conlin

Heave
The Memento

watermark

STORIES

christy ann conlin

Published in Canada in 2019 and the USA in 2019 by House of Anansi Press Inc.
www.houseofanansi.com

Permission is gratefully acknowledged to reprint excerpts from the following:

(Page 91) excerpt from *Mystery and Manners* by Flannery O'Connor, edited by Sally and
Robert Fitzgerald. Copyright © 1969 by the estate of Flannery O'Connor. Reprinted by
permission of Farrar, Straus and Giroux.

(Pages 253–264) passages from *Letters from a Stoic* by Seneca translated by Robin Alexander
Campbell (Penguin Classics, 1987).

(Page 267) excerpt from "The Love Song of J. Alfred Prufrock" from COLLECTED POEMS
1909–1962 by T. S. Eliot. Copyright © 1936 by Houghton Mifflin Harcourt Publishing
Company, renewed 1964 by Thomas Stearns Eliot. Reprinted by permission of Houghton
Mifflin Harcourt Publishing Company. All rights reserved. Permission also granted by Faber
and Faber Ltd.

Part title artwork borrowed from *Hamonshū* v. 3, by Mori Yūzan; Yamada Geisōdō,
Kyōto-shi, Meiji 36 [1903] / *Public Domain Review*

Every reasonable effort has been made to contact the holders of copyright for materials
quoted in this work. The publishers will gladly receive information that will enable them to
rectify any inadvertent errors or omissions in subsequent editions.

House of Anansi Press is committed to protecting our natural environment. As part of our
efforts, this book is made of material from well-managed FSC®-certified forests, recycled
materials, and other controlled sources.

23 22 21 20 19   1 2 3 4 5

Library and Archives Canada Cataloguing in Publication

Conlin, Christy Ann, author
Watermark / Christy Ann Conlin.

Short stories.
Issued in print and electronic formats.
ISBN 978-1-4870-0343-2 (softcover).—ISBN 978-1-4870-0344-9 (EPUB).—
ISBN 978-1-4870-0345-6 (Kindle)

I. Title.

PS8555.O5378W38 2019   C813'.6   C2018-906702-0
C2018-906703-9

Library of Congress Control Number: 2019930409

Book design: Alysia Shewchuk

Canada Council
for the Arts

Conseil des Arts
du Canada

ONTARIO ARTS COUNCIL
CONSEIL DES ARTS DE L'ONTARIO
an Ontario government agency
un organisme du gouvernement de l'Ontario

NOVA SCOTIA
NOUVELLE-ÉCOSSE

*We acknowledge for their financial support of our publishing program the Canada Council for the
Arts, the Ontario Arts Council, and the Government of Canada.*

Printed and bound in Canada

MIX
Paper from
responsible sources
FSC® C004071
www.fsc.org

In Friendship
for Sarah Emsley
&
In memorium for Maggie Estep
1963–2014
RIP

CONTENTS

Eyeball in Your Throat / 1

Dead Time / 23

The Diplomat / 69

Full Bleed / 89

Occlusion / 115

Late and Soon / 147

Back Fat / 165

Insomnis / 203

Desire Lines / 213

Beyond All Things Is the Sea / 249

The Flying Squirrel Sermon / 265

Acknowledgements / 301

EYEBALL IN YOUR THROAT

"EAT ANY EYEBALLS LATELY?"

Declan thought that was so funny. Lucy waited for him to finish laughing on the upstairs phone so she could hear what Deirdre was calling to tell them this time. Jesus Christ, when was he going to get over that inside joke? Lucy rocked in her chair, waiting while her daughter and husband rambled on. That Deirdre... always calling to tell, not ask. Declan was on the upstairs extension and Lucy on the kitchen phone, the same black rotary wall phone which had been in the old farmhouse when they first started renting it years ago.

"It's good to hear from you, *Deirdre an Bhróin.*" Lucy couldn't stand it when Declan tried to say their daughter's name as if it were Declan himself who'd just stepped off the boat, not his drunken papist grandparents. Declan insisted on naming their daughter Deirdre, not something pretty like Rose or Heather, which Lucy had preferred. He didn't even mention until Deirdre was starting school how the name came from a morbid Irish myth: Deirdre of the Sorrows.

Lucy remembered when Deirdre had been a small child, sweet and tender, laughing when she poured out her Corn Flakes and got a bowl of mouse turds instead. She laughed about everything back then instead of screaming as she did once she turned thirteen, when it was as if puberty had disturbed some slumbering animal inside her. David was such an easy child, spending most of his childhood reading books in the tree house Declan built in the woods by the stream. But not Deirdre. She was the one hanging from the branches by her knees, chattering and howling like a monkey with her long red hair flickering like flames as she swung.

Now here Lucy was trying to have a normal phone chat with her daughter, but a normal conversation with Deirdre was always impossible because she was never doing normal things. Like when she was little, coming home from the park with some story about the boogie man in the trees who chased her, and the neurotic little girl from the Lupin Cove Road she played with back then who grew to leave her fiancé at the altar so she could go to Europe. At least Lucy hadn't had to deal with something like that... yet. Lucy licked her lips and took a deep breath before she spoke.

"So how are you?"

"Oh I'm pretty good. Pretty good."

"I see. Cold up there?"

"Well, the river just broke."

Declan spoke. He was always asking questions about the wrong things, not making any effort to help Deirdre be normal and fit in. "When'd the Churchill River go and break?"

"The other day."

"That so. Like yesterday?"

"Beginning of June."

"Always break then?"

"Bit early this year."

"What did you say the Inuit call Churchill? I was trying to remember the other day so I could tell the fellas at the Blomidon Naturalists Society. *Koogie*..."

"*Kuugjuaq*. Dad. Churchill's the name the white people gave it. Hudson Bay is *Kangiqsualuk ilua*. The Cree there call the Churchill River *Missinipi*."

"Isn't that something? I'd love to come up and visit you in *Kuug-ju-aq*, Deirdre. See the Aurora Borealis. What did you say it's called?"

"*Arsaniit*. Well, look, Dad, actually...I thought I'd come home for the summer."

Home? Oh, God, that was it. This was why Deirdre was calling. Lucy could feel her anger wrapping around her like a shroud, suffocating her. Her chest tightened. She could hardly breathe. It was happening more and more, these surges of anger choking off her breath whenever she talked to her daughter. There was something beneath the anger, something quiet and desperate, poking at her insides. And Declan going on like he'd actually go up north to that godforsaken place. He was master of daydreams just as he was when they first met. She was a fool to think anything would ever come of those dreams. Deirdre was just like her father: a lush full of fantasies with the curse on her name.

"Well, that would be fine by me. We could go fishing on the river. We haven't done that since you were little, and David never had any interest. *Jijuktu'kwejk.* That's what the Mi'kmaq call it."

"I know. I'd love to go fishing. I really want to come home."

"Do you now?" Even Lucy's tongue was stiff and she could barely quiz her daughter.

"Yeah. Get back to work on my thesis. Help out in the garden maybe. Go fishing with Dad."

"That so? Is our job not working out up there in Churchill? Or in whatever the other name for that place is. I can't be expected to learn a foreign language at my age."

Silence.

Deirdre taking a breath.

"Yup. Finishing up."

Lucy always asked the right kinds of questions, not

6

like Declan, always encouraging Deirdre's ridiculous choices, always wanting to hear about whatever outlandish place she was in or silly job she had taken. Lucy had to redirect her or Deirdre would just tell them whatever she wanted, always giving bits and pieces which never made sense. She'd started doing this, making up stories to frighten Lucy, when she was a child and then she kept going as a teen. It was the teen years when it all went wrong, when Lucy could make neither head nor tail of Deirdre's stories. Lucy felt as if she were an intruder in her daughter's life when she spun her tales.

One day Deirdre stopped volunteering anything, saying Lucy only heard what she wanted to. From that day on her convoluted stories were reduced to bullet points. Like the eyeball. Deirdre said she flew into Rankin Inlet, that little Inuit village, and had a good time and ate lots of unusual stuff. Lucy asked what she meant by "unusual stuff" and Deirdre said weird stuff out of the sea and Lucy had to say *what the hell do you mean weird goddamn stuff out of the sea, can you be specific?* Then, and only then, did Deirdre share the details. Eating a seal eyeball—it was a real delicacy, she told them, an honour to be given one, and a test.

"What did it taste like?" Declan had been fascinated.

"An eyeball."

"Oh for Christ's sake, Deirdre, how the hell do you know what an eyeball tastes like? Lord God Almighty.

So if I pulled out my own eyeball and took a bite, it'd taste just like seal eyeball?"

Pause.

"Like fish oil."

Declan loved that, thought it was dandy, and told everybody at the square dancing on Wednesday night how his daughter was on the Hudson Bay eating seal eyeballs that tasted just like cod liver oil. Except he kept trying to say it how they did up there in that frozen wasteland, *Kangiqsualuk ilua*. He was as proud as she was embarrassed. Lucy almost walked out. It was so humiliating how Declan tried repeating the word over and over as they danced on the creaking wooden floor of the community hall. He'd sounded like he was having a hemorrhagic attack. And there was Erma doing an allemande left in her extra-full crinoline, her daughter an accountant and married with two kids. Alfretta over there doing a do-si-do, with her new dye job (Harvest Wheat Blonde), her daughter a dentist and married. And there was Lucy weaving-the-ring with her grey-streaked black hair, wilted crinoline, and her daughter eating eyeballs up in the North, not even working but *volunteering* with a bunch of nuns and learning to speak Inuktitut. It didn't even sound believable.

Declan and Deirdre kept jabbering away on the phone. Lucy looked out the window while Declan asked about the polar bears, the ice floes, the tundra, and all that sort of *National Geographic* stuff. Lucy herself had never fit in as a child and her ambition had been to see to it that her children did. She had failed there, that was for sure. Despite Lucy's best efforts over the years, all her daughter valued was gallivanting all over the earth, more interested in meeting people who offered her seal eyeballs than in settling down and having a regular life.

Lucy looked at the garden hose outside, leaning against the bird feeder. It was long and green, a handsome hose, coiled like a snake, complete with a power-pressure Garden King nozzle from the hardware store, seven different settings from Irish Mist to Northern Blast. Declan had given it to her for Mother's Day along with a lovely card he bought at the drug store. Lucy'd put the card on her dresser and hooked the nozzle up as soon as the warm weather had come. They had put the garden in after the planting moon. She treasured this about Declan, how he was one of those husbands who appreciated her efforts to mother, unlike Deirdre who didn't appreciate a single thing Lucy did.

Lucy had had no choice but to take the garden hose to Deirdre all those years ago. No matter how much things settled down, Deirdre was always there reminding her of every mistake she had ever made, always demanding Lucy make some sort of atonement for her wicked parenting. Lucy had decided to show her daughter just what kind of ritual would set things right, what sort of spell was needed to force Deirdre to see it was she who should be making amends and changing her ways, not blaming her mother for every single thing. There was only so much a mother could be expected to do. Lucy had found that there came a time when there was nothing to lose by acting like a witch since her own daughter always made her feel like one anyway.

Early one morning when Deirdre was twenty years old and home from university for the summer working in the pie factory down the road, Lucy found her face down in the yellow roses at dawn. Her long red hair was caught like seaweed on the thorns of the rose bush they had planted on her thirteenth birthday, vomit hanging off the delicate petals, clinging to the long pieces of Deirdre's hair, sun bouncing off the strands and scattering rays of red and mahogany, shattered in places by the gloppy vomit. Lucy had come around the corner of the house that morning, sat down on the verandah, taken a sip of coffee, and looked at her toes in the dewy grass. She saw Deirdre's hand flopped there on the front lawn.

The smell of vomit and sweet rose hanging thick on the hot June morning air reminded her of the funeral home. Lucy'd had a flash of standing by the coffin, looking at her father, dead from the booze at sixty, though they all liked to say it was the heart disease that killed him. But Lucy was beginning to see it was your life that killed you — in the end it was how you lived that took you out. Life shaped your heart and it killed you.

So there lay her daughter face down in the rose garden, all sprawled out in her outrageous beauty with her face in the dry, well-weeded earth. Her drool was soaking a dark pool by her cheek. This is how she'd landed on her way home at God knows what time from another booze-soaked late-night party.

Lucy had put the coffee down and pulled the hose around. She'd pressed the lever and let rip with a furious blast of water, at first hot from lying in the sun in the rubber hose and then freezing cold as it came from deep below the ground, from the well out back they had dug when they'd stopped renting the place. The water smashed down on Deirdre's head and back and legs. She thrashed like a centipede. She rolled over a few times and then sat up on the grass, long wet hair plastered to her cheeks, a freak screaming as though her outrage would make the water stop, dirt and vomit dripping down her nose, mouth open like a tunnel. Lucy let blast right inside her dirty mouth, pounding Deirdre's face clean and drowning her cries, drowning her fury.

Declan opened an upstairs window and poked his head out, followed by David at his bedroom window to see what was happening so early on Saturday morning. And they had hung there like gargoyles watching Deirdre jump to her feet, screaming at her mother, *You're killing me! You're killing me!*

And Lucy screaming back, *I'm gonna have a heart attack. I'm gonna have a heart attack. You're killing me with your stupid life. What about my life? Doesn't a mother count?*

And Declan bellowing, *Can't you girls just stop it? Can't we just have a nice morning?*

David rolling his eyes and going back to bed.

Lucy had followed Deirdre over the lawn with the hose as she staggered in circles, putting her hands on her body as her mother shot her with the water, screaming for her to stop but not leaving, not running into the house or down the driveway to the highway and hitching into the city like she had done before. Not this time. She was dancing around like a kite on a string, the water the current that moved her.

Lucy had let go the lever, the water instantly disappearing and Deirdre's screams with it. The wrath that had boiled up in Lucy just as quickly settled, leaving her weak and trembling, as though the tide had come barrelling in with each wave tossing cumbersome years on her shoulders before it receded and left her so weighted. Her heart pounded as though it was trying to leave her body. She and her daughter stood like lawn ornaments, staring at each other, the morning birds chirping loud and clear in the sudden silence, a cow mooing in the pasture.

Deirdre seemed to shrink into a little girl, that same little girl who'd come home from the park crying, disturbing little stories coming off her lips, stories Lucy didn't want to hear. Lucy rubbed her eyes and put her hand on her chest, catching her breath. A slight breeze had come up, and Lucy had watched her daughter's skin go bumpy and cold in the already hot June day, wondering where she had gone wrong or if it was just the genetics. It was the last summer Deirdre had come back from university—it was the last time she had come home.

Deirdre and Declan were still talking on the phone, Declan and his endless questions, each one leading to another obscurity or memory. Lucy's hands shook. It was hard enough remembering the early years but it was nothing compared to reliving those times after Deirdre became a teenager. All she did then was add complications to Lucy's already stressful life. Lucy hated thinking about how hard she had to work to crush Deirdre back into place, not that she'd stay there for long. Lucy felt like going outside, grabbing the hose, pulling it in the house, over the waxed floor and hooked rugs, and pounding it into the receiver, flooding the phone line with a powerful gush of water to pound some sense into her ignorant child. Deirdre still hadn't figured out that it's how you live that makes you happy in the end. The details. Being happy isn't about smiling all the time, partying 'til all hours and studying whatever you want in school, it's about appreciating what's been given to you.

"But I think I could come home, work on my thesis, get a little house, maybe . . . have a garden."

"Deirdre, you can't come home to nothing. You hate it here."

Silence.

"But you and Dad are there."

"Yes, we are here, and we've been here for our whole lives. You're thirty years old. And anyway, you can't plant a garden and just leave it."

Silence on the phone and then a dry sound as Deirdre swallowed.

"I can't stay up here."

A detail.

"Too cold is it?"

"Yeah. Too cold. I'm homesick."

Oh my. Details.

"You've just got to make a go of it."

"But I want to come home. I want to come home. Can't I make a go of it at home?"

"Well, you've spent your life since you were fifteen trying to get away from here. How do you think coming back is going to make it any better?"

"You did. You came back. You brought us all back."

"And many's the time I've wished I'd not come back, my girl."

Declan was standing in the doorway, watching her. He was giving them time to talk one on one, but she could tell he couldn't stand to listen to them fighting. Lucy looked at him and then away. It had been Declan's constant drinking way back then. How he couldn't hold a job. Everybody's goddamn boozing had been enough to make Lucy want a drink, though she never took to it the way all the drunks around her did. She just took to the garden. But Declan's drinking had stopped, and now he stood there in the doorway nervously, watching Lucy say goodbye to Deirdre, watching her hang up the phone and sit there staring out the window.

Later Lucy saw him watching her from the window while she worked in the garden, and she saw him come out holding her sun hat, and she felt his shadow as he stood over her.

"Should wear this, Dear." He placed the straw hat on her head and she didn't flinch. "I got some work around here she can do, Luce. And David won't be home this summer, all the way over there in Africa with Médecins Sans Frontières." Lucy adjusted the hat and pulled out a weed as she listened to Declan butcher the French words.

"All the way over in Africa doing the volunteer

work," she said. "Lord. Declan, doesn't anyone make a salary anymore? Everyone working for free these days?" She waited for him to justify why their children were so different from their friends' children.

"Aren't a lot of jobs out there now, Luce. You know that."

Lucy pulled out another weed. She was very tired. It was as though the disappointment of her entire life was trying to press her down into the earth. "What's she going to do around here?" Lucy's voice was barely a whisper and Declan answered in a gentle tone, as if he were trying to match her voice and keep hers from rising.

"Lots of stuff. You know I can't do what I could before, what with the bursitis. Lots of stuff, the house needs painting or we're going to have to take off them shingles and put on the siding."

"You know how I hate the siding." Luey yanked out a fistful of weeds but the effort to pull them felt like she had ploughed an entire field by hand. It was stifling hot, worse than normal.

"I know you hate the siding, and that's why we have to keep the paint on the wood so the rot don't get in. If you want to live in an old house, then you got to do the upkeep. Deirdre could help out with all this, all the stuff Davie used to do."

"I'm not moving into a bungalow. I may be retired,

but I am not moving into a bungalow." Lucy sat down on the lawn.

"Lucy, the sun's too bright for you."

He went in and came out with some pink lemonade and peanut butter cookies, and they sat in the shade together, watching the hummingbirds sipping at the nectar in the trumpet honeysuckle. There were more hummingbirds than ever this year. Over two dozen. Declan counted them every morning and every evening. They hardly ever alighted, constantly feeding, drawn to the exotic beauty around them.

"Dec, that's a fine feeder you've hung up there."

Lucy watched Declan as he sipped his lemonade and peered up into the sky, tracing the birds with his pinkie finger.

"I know you're not moving into a bungalow, Lucy. I'm not saying that—"

"Then what are you saying, Declan? What are you trying to say?"

"Well, if you let me finish, I'd say it."

"Well, say it."

"I'm saying let Deirdre come home and help us out around here, for the summer."

A bird hummed by Lucy's head. She didn't know where it had all gone wrong, why every year passed and yet she never felt happy, why her family was always letting her down.

"And then what?"

"Well, then she's got her master's in linguistics now, don't she? She's not just a walking mess of problems. The girl speaks five languages. That's something, Lucy."

Lucy wiped her forehead. "Yes, Lord yes, it is, I'm not going to argue about that. She's just got her frigging thesis she can't finish. But they all got their master's these days. They're either volunteering or working in a café. No one does anything normal anymore. Deirdre went and learned languages hardly anyone speaks. How practical is that?" Lucy was yelling now, almost crying.

"If she wants to learn languages hardly anyone speaks that's something we should be proud of. How many people around here would even bother? There's just no pleasing you. Lucy, God almighty, if she wants to come, then let her come home. She never wanted to come home before."

It was true, Lucy thought. Deirdre never *had* wanted to come before. Not through the detox, the hospital, the unemployment, the welfare, the in and out of university, all the endless breakups with one man after another. Lucy could never keep their names straight. Just a spattering of phone calls, sometimes drunk ones in the middle of the night, sometimes hung-over calls in the middle of the afternoon, never after supper or on Sunday when most people called. They'd been phoned and told item by item, no details.

I'm off the booze.

Went to detox.

Went to rehab.

Learned a new language.

Going to university.

Graduated.

Broke up with Matthew the lawyer, Reverend John, Jason the guitarist, Charles the interpreter, Professor Patrick the leprechaun, and the Pied-Bloody-Piper.

Learned another new language.

Started my master's.

Dropped out of my master's.

Met Dr. Bob.

Going up north to work with the Grey Nuns.

Learned Inuktitut.

Broke up with Dr. Bob.

Canoed on the river with migrating beluga whales.

Ate an eyeball.

Any time Lucy wanted, she could sit down in the comfy chair on the verandah, shut her eyes, smell the roses, and think back to the vomit. It was easy to imagine Deirdre in a coffin in the funeral home, just like her grandfather, all laid out and done in by her heart. And Lucy could scatter pieces of her own heart on the grave. She told Declan that Deirdre could come home.

LUCY AND DECLAN WERE in the shade having iced tea, escaping the high noon sun, when the car came down the driveway. It was almost six weeks since the horrible eyeball phone call. July was always a stunning month, a month you could count on. The roses were in full bloom, the raspberries were on, and the blue sky hung over like a stretch of lake. Lucy was exhausted again. The heat had never bothered her this much.

Deirdre had written a letter mentioning she was going to arrive this Sunday, but of course, didn't say how or when. Just said she didn't need to be picked up at the airport, and Lucy didn't ask any questions. These days she was too tired to think about the particulars, asking the right kinds of questions. At square dancing last week she hadn't even noticed the others, and she could hardly follow the calls, turning the wrong way, getting dizzy when Declan would swing her, not able to even do a grand chain without losing her breath. Lucy just wanted to sit in the shade and watch the humming-birds feasting.

But there she was, Deirdre, in a little beat-up lime-coloured car, back seat packed full of boxes. And there Deirdre was looking all old and grown up. Funny how you always remember them as little—Deirdre sitting barefoot at the table, laughing at the bowl full of mouse turds. When Lucy's own mother was dying five years back, she would cry out *Oh my little girl* to Lucy. And now here was her own daughter looking like she was an adult, all big and round in her stomach, a detail she of course hadn't offered and what must have brought her home. Little lines by Deirdre's mouth, by her eyes, on her forehead. Lucy hoped they were laugh lines. She understood then Deirdre was home for some love, love Lucy had never been able to give her, or anyone.

It is then Lucy feels a tight pain in her heart. Her daughter standing by the car door, smiling and walking over to her, moving slowly over the grass, running awkwardly as Lucy falls down in the sweet roses. Thorns piercing her arms as she gasps for a breath which does not come, choking on the honeyed details she finally tastes and savours, her eyes closing and flickers of green and white becoming a veil against the horizon of her mind as Declan and Deirdre's voices blur and are lost in the beating of a thousand luminous hummingbird wings.

DEAD TIME

GUILTY, GUILTY, GUILTY THEIR eyes all say, the words scratching themselves into the concrete walls. Beige. It's the worst colour. So boring. So flat, just like all the people around me, like the life they want to force me into. But I am the consort of scarlet fire beings and sirens of the blue ice. The bland brittle world my captors exist in will never hold me, will never break me. In my mind I stand gazing upon the tall marble palace looming over a glittering sea that lashes and whips the unbreakable twilight. The exploding sun and the molten moon are infused in my blood. Through the grey mists and streaks of lavender smoke I alone see what stands in the turret and looks down upon me with glowing eyes, eyes the deep aqua of a cunning ocean which holds all the mystery and darkness of the world.

But these bland walls, where their judgment latches

itself, this beige revolts me. The whole penal institution is this colour. That's what this place is, a penitentiary, even though they call it a *youth centre*, like it's a community club — a locked club with bars on the windows.

But I'm telling you, I'm not guilty. There was nothing I could do once Sergei started. He would have killed me. He was in a rage, and all I could do was scream.

I'M SITTING HERE WITH my father. He's not saying a word. He looks exhausted. His skin is shades of dirty beige except for around his eyes where it's yellow and green, as though he hasn't slept in days. He's like a snake, so it wouldn't surprise me if he could go for days without food or sleep, just slithering about behind people. That's the kind of man he is. He hasn't shaved and his fingers stroke the stubble on his chin and he puts his face in his hands. He's totally wrapped up in his career as a politician, calling the shots, the backroom deals. I know the kind of people who live in that world, obsessed with themselves, monsters creeping toward the manger.

That's what the youth worker accused me of when I got here. Being *obsessed* with myself. Can you believe it? We were in the dining hall, and I said I wasn't going to eat the dried-out mashed potatoes from a box.

"The food sucks in here," I said in a loud voice. Well,

didn't that fat youth worker at the end of the table tell me to be quiet. I was so pissed off.

She was standing right over me. And she laughed. I couldn't believe it, like I was a big joke. *No one* laughs at me.

"Yes, Isabella, I can tell you what to do. And I'll tell you it would be smart to stop obsessing over yourself and what you want. Think about other people for a change. Maybe the girl who died. The girl they say you killed. Maybe think about her for once."

Her. Lulu. Like I wanted to think about *her*.

MY FATHER STILL ISN'T speaking. Time is crawling by but there is a clock in here and I know it's only been a few minutes. His face is still in his hands. He needs to cut his fingernails. He hasn't had time for that either. My mind is galloping, a wild horse tearing through my past, through my life, showing me every horrible thing that has ever happened, all those crazy people who have tried to pull me down.

It was Lulu, Sergei's stupid ex, who caused all these problems in the first place, starting the day we saw her at the store. Lulu didn't go to the same school as us, and I never really thought much about her until that day when we were buying Popsicles. She was tiny, with long hair, a ruby-red nose stud. "Hi, Sergei," she said in this cutesy voice, looking down at her feet and then looking up. She didn't even wait for him to say hello, just walked out. Right before she did she winked at him, right in front of me, a sexy wink with her long eyelashes, all coy.

What nerve. Winking was *our* thing. How we got together. I'm the one who winks at Sergei, not *her*. She's not winking these days, now, is she?

I was watching him all the time after that. Sergei denied it, said she didn't wink. Like he thought I was blind. How insulting. It was so obvious. He said Lulu was really shy; she wouldn't do something like that. I didn't talk to him all the way home, and when he parked the car in my driveway, he told me not to be jealous. I wanted to stick a fork in him then. Of course I was jealous — but I wasn't going to let him know. Who did he think he was to accuse *me* of being jealous of *her*? I made myself laugh, like I didn't care. "Why would I be jealous? You dumped her," I said with my eyes almost closed.

His hands got tight on the steering wheel and the yellow skin on the side of his index finger from all the weed he smokes was bright against the black vinyl. "So?" he said.

Lulu. Who did she think she was that she could just wink and come on to my boyfriend? Like I was invisible, like I was some stand-in for her.

MAYBE MY FATHER IS sleeping. Maybe time has stopped and the clock has been slowed and he can't move his head from his hands. Maybe we've been pushed into a time warp. But I'm not going to say anything, just sit here with my arms crossed and wait for the warp to shift or for my father to lift up his head and face me.

Just like that stupid youth worker who stood looking down at me, like she thought I was going to suddenly say I was guilty or something. I could feel my heart going *boom-banga-boom-boom* and then I just lost it. I stood up and threw my mashed potatoes right in her pudgy face, plate and all. Well, they came from everywhere, the youth workers, throwing me to the floor, arms behind my back, and they carried me like I was an Egyptian mummy into the cell they insisted on calling my room, in this stupid effort to have us think we were at a resort or a vacation camp. They took out everything and left me there on the concrete floor. Bastards. I was so mad. Who do they think they are that they can do this to me? They sent in the officer-in-charge for the night, and he told me I was lucky the youth worker wasn't going to charge me with assault.

"For throwing a plastic plate of mashed potatoes?" I said to him. I rolled my eyes. "Come on. It's not like she didn't deserve it."

"You can't even see how it's wrong, can you?" He looked like he was feeling sorry for me, but not because

I was trapped in here, but as though he believed I was some heartless freak. His pager went off and then he left, but not before looking at me and shaking his head. I'd like to give him a shake.

I hate them all. They keep telling me I need to work on my attitude, honesty is important, taking responsibility is important, like they think I'm a liar. I have no problem telling them where they can shove their comments, because who the hell are they to talk down to me?

THE TIME WARP SHIFTS. My father stands up. He needs to use the washroom. He knocks on the door and some guard comes and opens it. He says he'll be right back. I'm alone in the beige.

It's been three months I've been sitting in here. It took three weeks for my throat to stop aching from screaming at Sergei. *Just let her go.* He didn't have to prove anything to me. He turned on me then. The bruises on my face have faded now. At first they turned green and red as though I'd rubbed my cheek on some weird plant in a pond deep in a forest, some magic pond. Bad magic. In fairy tales girls like me turn the magic around. The heroines always take control. The sky erupts and terrifying smoke of pink and purple slinks down and around the girl's wrists and pulls her up, and she becomes giant, looming over them all, her laugh a million smashing thunderbolts which rip and shred her foes into pieces.

I press my lips together, lips that would feel better with lipstick, but there is no lipstick in this place. No nail polish. It's all about pale here, washed-out walls, dull carpets. Boring colours that don't tell you anything. You can't trust beige.

It will take a long time to move past all of this, everything that has happened, the way they are treating me in here. My father says I'll need a lot of counselling. He says the police say I did it, but my lawyer is going to demand that I be released once they give Sergei's statement to the court, saying that he was the one. My lawyer's going to tell the judge I have post-traumatic stress disorder from watching Sergei murder that girl. PTSD. It sounds like the name of a band.

The door opens. The warden is old, almost fifty, I bet, older than my dad. There is no kindness in his blue eyes. There's something else in there, but I haven't figured out what it is yet. I will. But he's got a shield up. He's seen it all, he tells me whenever he meets with me.

They act like everyone in here is guilty, even me, on remand, with no trial yet. The warden says he knows I'm afraid, it's normal, but I need to show respect. I can't yell at the staff. I can't throw things. It doesn't matter how angry I get, how upset; there are appropriate ways to behave, and I'll be in here for a lot longer if I don't behave.

"Even if they're rude to *me*?" I ask him. "If they don't show me respect?"

"Expecting you to do what they say, when they say it, isn't rude," he says.

"You don't know what it's like to be locked up."

"No," he says, "I don't. You should have thought of that before."

"But I didn't do anything," I tell him.

The warden nods. "Yes, so you say."

I look away. He doesn't care that I'm a victim too. He thinks because my father is a politician I feel entitled to special treatment. I don't.

"They'll be here for you soon," he says. Maybe my father isn't coming back. I don't even bother asking. I won't give him the satisfaction of knowing I want to know what's going on. He leaves and I look at the door as he walks out.

Click.

The sharp sound of the door locking fills the cell and then fades into a dream sound, a muffled, faraway echoing.

Click, click.

My mother used to tap her shoe when she wanted something done. She'll have been gone for three years this spring, and I can still hear the *click* her high heels made on the ceramic tile.

Click when the door closed behind her. The *click* the phone made when she'd hang up when we'd have our weekly call after she left and moved. She always said she had to hang up before I was ready to stop talking. Then I would hear the sound of the call ending.

Clickity clack, I'm not coming back.

"It's not you," she said, during our first call. "It's me." Like she was breaking up with me. "It's always been my dream to live in a house on the beach with palm trees. And be with someone who's home more often than not." And someone half her age—she didn't mention that.

Snap. My father flipping his phone shut.

Snap, snap, snickity snap. We don't need her, shut her trap.

Twelve years old is more than old enough, he said. You're old enough to babysit. We'll manage. Let her have her palm trees.

And then he was off to work, before I was even dressed to go out and wait for the school bus.

Beep. His car started with a flick of his button.

Click. The garage door opened. Off he drove.

Click. I shut the door to the house.

The walls of our house were beige then. Sable, my mother called them. Sable, she would say, picking up a crystal hourglass she had, *tawny, sandy, sandy dune, sparkling in the sun of June,* turning it upside down on the table by the window where the afternoon sun spilled in, watching every grain drift down.

THE DOORKNOB TURNS. The door slams open. I only see the arm of the guard and then my father comes back in. He sits down. I wait for him to talk but he doesn't even say anything, just sighs. I'm not going to be the one who says anything. I'm not going to open my mouth and let that beige flood down my throat and invade my body.

It's hard to keep track of time in here. Every day is like the other. I've been to court twice already. They cuff me and shackle me. Strip search me when I come back. Like I'm a common criminal. My hands keep sweating. I don't know why. I'm not nervous or any-thing. Sergei said he'd tell them, and I know they'll drop the charges. I don't know why it's taking them so long to check out his story.

I told him, when we were waiting there by the pond for the police to come, if he didn't say it, if he tried to blame me, I would tell them where his grow op was, his big marijuana patch, and they'd take his house away and then his grandmother, the old wrinkled babushka that he worships, would have nowhere to live and

they'd stick her in a nursing home. They always con-
fiscate drug property, don't they? I said I'd tell them he
forced me to have sex with him even though it's not
true. I told him if he really loved me, if he wanted to
prove his love, then he would be a man and say he did
it—true love is about proving your love.

I mean, he has to take responsibility, and I'm not
beyond forcing him to. I told it all to the police, what
happened to his ex-girlfriend. They went over and over
the story with me, and I told them the same thing every
time. You didn't help him? they asked. You didn't drown
her? I started to cry then. How could they think I would
do that? She fell in the pond. I couldn't reach her. It was
too deep.

This whole thing is her fault, Sergei's fault. When
we started seeing each other he never talked about
her—I never knew a thing about her until the day we
were at the store getting Popsicles and cigarettes and
she was at the cash paying. She looked up and smiled,
at him, not me. That's when the trouble started.

Sergei will do the right thing. *Or else*, I told him.
He made all of this happen. I keep going over and
over what happened, because it's easy to get the story
mixed up.

It's like it's a comic book. I can see it in my mind
whether my eyes are open or shut. It was so confusing
at first, trying to remember, because it happened so

35

fast. But then I remembered, piece by piece, picture by picture. I told the police how Sergei just went crazy. He was fanatical when it came to proving his love for me, and he was fixated on getting rid of her. I wanted to help Lulu, but I was scared of doing anything because he was so out of control. I realized he was crazy and maybe it could have been me lying in the lily pond, not her. Just a snap of the fingers and our roles reversed. I wish it *was* me, I told my father and the police. I wish it was me and not her who had to suffer, I said with my voice cracking. I couldn't believe how upset I sounded. My father's eyes filled up with tears and he said in a very kind voice that I wasn't responsible for Sergei and what he did, and I shouldn't blame myself.

BEING LOCKED UP IS probably harder on other kids in here than it is on me. I'm used to being on my own, because my father is always working. Except for now, when he's visiting me, but just sitting there with his hands over his eyes, like he's sleeping sitting up, or try-ing to punish me with his silence.

I'm also used to doing what I want, and that's what's hard in here. I can't piss unless they authorize it. When I first realized they were going to charge me, I lost it. I was screaming and crying and this youth worker did what they call "non-violent crisis intervention." Those words, "youth worker" — what a joke. She's a guard. They should just be honest about this. I'm a prisoner. It's a prison. I don't know why they have to make up all this language to hide the truth. Who do they think they're fooling?

There is a tiny window with bars embedded in the glass — it's a *state of the art* facility. The window faces east and I can see a bit of the sky beyond. The sky is magenta as the sun comes up. They bring me breakfast in here on a tray and I get to look at the wall while I await transport to the courthouse, going over and over what happened, wondering what will be next.

MY FATHER CAME TO see me less than an hour after I was arrested. It feels like an eon ago, not three months ago. The first thing I noticed was the stubble on his face. Something had finally shaken his world up, like he was a little man in a snow globe who'd become unglued from the bottom and was now floating around banging his head on the plastic walls, trying to get his feet glued back down again. He came in and he looked at me, his eyes all red. "Isabella. What happened? You have to tell me." I had my arms crossed and he leaned over and took my hand. It was the first time he'd touched me tenderly since I was ten years old, aside from patting me on the shoulder like I was the dog.

It's a long drive for him, but he's been coming twice a week. It could be a disaster for his career, although he hasn't said this, which is unusually thoughtful of him. I've seen my father more than I ever did when we lived in the same house. He must like the routine here. He's all about routine. Every Sunday is visitor time, although they've made some special arrangements for him to have an extra visit.

They do art therapy in here. Mandatory art. What's therapeutic about that? I ask the art instructor. Her name is Elaine. It's printed on the red facility pass she has clipped to her smock, the pass that gives her access to the high security part of the facility. Her name is pronounced like it's *élan*, like she thinks she's from Paris or something, instead of just some bitch from the boring world. She keeps correcting us when we get it wrong. I always say it wrong to see what she'll do. I'd like to come up behind *Élan*, grab her stupid ponytail and give a yank and watch her neck snap. That would be pretty funny live art.

SOMEONE CALLED HER "Elaine-the-Shit-Stain" to see what she would do. She just smiled and finally said, "Call me whatever you want, I don't care." All the girls laughed. They don't have anything else to do but laugh. They have sentences already.

I'm the only one in here on remand, on dead time, waiting for my dumb court date. The stupid youth workers told me they've seen other people sit in here for a year waiting for their trial, next they're found guilty and none of it counts as time served, a whole year of dead time.

Elaine comes every week. She's the only one in here who is nice, who doesn't talk down to me. Art is the only thing I can stand. I want to be an interior designer. My father wanted our whole house redone, and he let me choose the colours.

Yesterday in art therapy Elaine got us to pick colours to reflect how we feel. She has this colour wheel she uses, a poster she puts on the wall. Colour therapy, she calls it. All the shades of purple spoke to me. I touched each one of them, the lavender and plum, the mauve and lilac, the pale violets and the deep wines, the grape and heather purples. "Yes," she said, smiling. "What does it say about you, this colour?"

What I thought then and will always believe is this: I am all the colours of the sunrise and sunset, painted by a dark demon spirit who dwells in a stone tower on a cliff which looks out over a dark blue sea where only mermaids who have betrayed their kind now swim with sharks and strange monsters of the deep who never come to the surface. But I didn't say that. I just smiled and looked down. When I looked up, she was staring at me, her eyes these pale green pools, the pupils dark lilies.

"You can always talk to me, Isabella. About anything. I know you don't talk to the other girls and you've had some trouble with the youth workers. It's hard having to be polite all the time. You must feel very alone." She smiled all friendly.

I could feel the panic crawling up my throat then, like some sort of horrible lizard. My eyes filled up with tears, but I didn't say anything because I learned long ago people don't really care, and I wasn't about to trust her even though she seemed like she really felt bad for me — but it's all pretend, just like the rotten tooth fairy and that sort of shit. This is what growing up is about, learning how adults just lie their heads off.

And it's not just the lies. It's something beneath that, something flat and insubstantial about how they are inside. It's like they aren't real. It's pretend how humans grow up and mature, have meaning in their lives. It makes me want to barf. This morning when I woke up I imagined a shelf running along the top of the cell with the head of every adult who has ever caused me a problem sitting on it like a vase.

SERGEI ALWAYS SAID HE was a tough guy, I told the police. Talking about beating up losers. He was in court once for uttering death threats, so I know they'll believe me.

Sergei's grandfather was Russian, born and raised in Moscow when it was the Soviet Union. Sergei told me that if his grandfather hadn't defected, Sergei could have been a Russian hockey star, because they have a better hockey program over there. At first I thought Sergei was telling the truth. He is so big, so strong. But he doesn't even speak Russian. And then I found out his grandfather wasn't a Russian spy. He was a janitor at the American embassy in Moscow. Apparently the embassy even let janitors defect. But I suppose everybody has secrets, even janitors.

The truth is, Sergei smoked away his hockey career. They told stories about him when I started high school last year. My father kept asking why I couldn't find a boy my own age. You're only fifteen, and he's nineteen. He can't even get out of high school. My father didn't understand how boys my own age are tedious. He told me he didn't want to see him anymore.

I kept my end of the bargain. He never did see him—because I only had Sergei over when my father wasn't at home.

But then, if my father was really concerned about me, he would have stayed around a bit more, wouldn't he? He can't fool me. His lack of concern reeks beneath the expensive aftershave he splashes on every morning.

He uses being an adult as an excuse so he can do as he pleases. What makes me so mad is he thinks because I'm so young I don't know. He thinks he's hiding in plain sight but he underestimates me. My grandmother died when I was little, but I remember she said when he was a boy he was always dressing up in a suit, staying inside to count his piggy bank when the other kids were outside climbing trees. When he married my mother they went on their honeymoon to a resort where he had a conference so he could use the trip as a tax write-off. She just sat on the beach the whole time, talking to cabana boys.

MY FATHER'S SECOND VISIT here, I came into the visiting cell and he looked up at me like he was going to chair a meeting. He had a pad of paper and a pen. "Tell me what happened. I'm getting you the best lawyer. I'll see Sergei is put away forever." He was talking really fast. He was all business, just writing notes, doing damage control. Clean-shaven. Not like the first time, when he still cared enough about me to be upset.

I said Sergei was going to tell them what really happened. He wasn't all bad, I told my father. I mean, who is all bad? Sergei wasn't going to let them put me away for something he was responsible for. He promised when the police arrived at the pond that he would make sure they knew the truth, how I was totally innocent. Sergei would keep his word.

My father nodded, playing with his pen. It drove me crazy that he wouldn't even look me in the eye. It was like he didn't believe a word I was saying.

But at least he didn't just sit there saying nothing, like he's doing now.

LULU WAS EVERYWHERE AFTER that time we saw her at the store. We drove by her once and she was walking her big white poodle, and she gave us a flutter of her hand and a smile, and of course, she winked. I could see her, even though we were driving fast. Sergei said there was no way I could have seen her from so far away, how I was starting to act crazy, really paranoid. Well, I could feel my face turn red when he said this.

"Crazy? Me, crazy?" And I put my hand on the door handle and opened the door. "Maybe I'll just hop out right here. How about that? I'm sure my father would love to know you pushed me out of the car." Of course I would never have jumped out but Sergei didn't know that, did he?

He slammed on the brakes. "Isabella, are you out of your mind?"

"I know exactly what I'm doing. Don't you dare

call me crazy. I'm not the one who's crazy for their ex-girlfriend, now am I?"

He said he wasn't, but how was I supposed to know if he was telling the truth?

I MISS SERGEI'S HANDS. Big, strong, warm. They were always warm on my body, moving so slowly. My Russian love machine, I called him. I can see his hands when I close my eyes, his hands open like fans, spread like sea stars on the sand.

He was always wanting me. But I only let him when he was good, when he behaved, when he did my chores around the house, when he arrived exactly when I told him to and left when I said so, when he called me exactly when I told him to. Then he'd get his reward.

I mean, he wasn't doing much with his life, just looking after his grandmother all the time, but anyone can look after an old Russian lady. What's the big deal? I told him he was a loser, that he'd let his life just rot. He got so angry, so hurt. He wanted to get married, but I told him I couldn't marry him like he was. And who gets married when they are fifteen? But Lulu, I bet she wanted to marry him. She would probably be into teen marriage, just to get her claws in him, to get Sergei away from me. She'd probably get pregnant right away and he'd be stuck with her for the rest of his life, and it would be just fine with her.

MY FATHER DIDN'T EVEN know Sergei and I were seeing each other, that's what he told the police. He'd forbidden it. He forbid a lot of things, but it's hard to rule the castle when you are never in the kingdom. That's what I told him when he came to see me here for the first time three months ago, after they called him and said I'd been arrested. I remember my father sitting there, all tired-looking, rumpled. We were in a little room and there was a youth worker sitting outside the door.

"But I told you not to see him anymore," he said, looking at the bruise on my face, putting his head in his hands.

"Yes, I know, Daddy. But I was lonely." I looked at him and then down again. It was easy to start crying. I used to practise in my bedroom with a stopwatch to see how quickly I could make my eyes tear. I would think about starving children in Africa, their bony bodies and bloated stomachs, things like that. I would sit on my bed, holding my pink princess mirror in one hand and the stopwatch in the other, and I would picture poor little children, all alone, children in those refugee camps with no parents, and then the tears would slip over my eyelids and run down my face. Just looking at myself was amazing, how my eyes filled up like fish bowls and the tears slid down in a perfect oval shape, how blue I looked. It was like watching a star in a movie, this really beautiful girl who no one understands and she's all alone all the time, her boyfriend's ex-girlfriend trying to steal him away.

After that I only had to picture my face and I could get the waterworks going right away. It took about sixty seconds at first, but I got it down to thirty seconds after doing it every day for a week. Just as the tears started to fall, I pushed up my sleeve again so my father could see the purple there too, where Sergei had grabbed me. Perfect timing.

My father looked up, but not at me, at the beige wall. There were tears in his eyes, and he couldn't stop them from coming out.

I REMEMBER ALL THOSE times in the front hall of our house, when my father would leave for evening meetings. He'd be on the way out the door and he'd say, "Now, Isabella, you do your homework. Stay off the phone. Don't be on the computer all night." I'd smile and he'd pat me on the cheek. *That's my girl.*

When he drove down the road I'd call Sergei and he'd come over. My father would always have these chores for me to do, mow the lawn, weed the garden. Sergei would do them while I sat in the lawn chair. It was nice living in the country, so much privacy living up on the Mountain. You could do whatever you wanted. When Sergei's back was turned I'd take my clothes off. He'd turn around and his eyes would pop and he'd run his tongue over his sexy red lips and give me this hot little smile.

I WAS SAD WHEN my mother left, but I was only twelve, and three years is enough time to get over it. She hated the house. It had been my father's idea to move to the country. He said the commute was worth the peace and quiet. But she was bored, sitting in the chair looking down over the field to the valley below. She bought a painting and hung it there by the big window. It was all these pastel swirls and had words on it: *Soft winter white makes pale winter blues.*

"Why are you going?" I'd asked her that day I got off the bus. My mother was in the doorway with her suitcases. It was June. She'd forgotten it was a half-day at school, and I came home to find her packing up her car.

"You'll be fine. You're just like him," she said as she got into the car, smiling at me. Not a mean smile. A smile like it was the only thing she could do and, even though it was such a small thing, she felt good about it.

She was gone but it didn't mean my father was around more. It was like nothing had changed for him.

I was in the city once, on a school trip. We got lost and we ended up at a hotel, a fancy one in the city centre. There was a café in the middle of the lobby with all these potted trees. You could have a drink there or afternoon tea in the hotel café. There was a woman sitting at a table and Susan, my classmate, whispered she was a hooker. She had dyed platinum hair and stiletto black boots. I suppose she could have been a hooker. We were sitting there and who came in and sat down with her but my father. Susan didn't know it was my father sitting there.

He didn't see me until we were leaving. I was outside on the sidewalk and he saw me through the glass wall. His eyes got huge. I just looked away and giggled with my friends as the bus pulled up for us. He got home late that night and I was already in bed. Of course I wasn't asleep but he didn't know that. He tried to bring it up the next day at breakfast but I just brushed him off and said I didn't care.

But I did care and I couldn't stop thinking about it. He had time to spend with her, some prostitute, but he never had time to spend with his own daughter. Just picturing her there with my father made me so mad. The nerve. Taking him away from me. I mean, she wouldn't be laughing if she was put in her place, would she? It would have served her right to have me come up to her, and she'd look at me, like I was going to ask a question, and then I'd take out a hammer, just a little one like the kind they use for reupholstering furniture, and give her whore head a whack and see how long she was able to stand up on her high heels then.

THE POLICE WANTED TO know how I hooked up with Sergei. That was the term they used, *hooked up*. I tried not to laugh.

I'd seen Sergei around at school. He kept to himself. He wasn't much into school, really, just goofing off. He might be a loser, but he's the best-looking loser around. He's really tall and he was in martial arts for a while too.

One day my dad dropped me off after an appointment with the orthodontist and Sergei was standing by the school door on the side having a cigarette. You aren't supposed to smoke on school property, but Sergei never cared about rules. I walked by and he smiled and then, with those big eyes of his, he winked. Well, I winked right back at him, with my head to the side all sexy, and just kept going. I know he turned and watched me walk away, so I made it worth his while.

I was grocery shopping with my father the day after and I saw Sergei in the parking lot loading groceries in the trunk of a car for this little old lady—his grand-mother, he told me later. And then I saw him driving by when I was out walking the dog. I was just coming home and turned in the driveway when he went by. He waved. I stood there looking at him. At the last second, I waved, and then I turned my head as he gave me this big smile.

The next day I walked by the north corner of the school where he hung out with the guys who always got in trouble, and he was leaning there against the wall and gave me his lazy smile again. "Why are you stalking me?" I said. He just laughed. And all his friends started laughing. But his laugh wasn't mean—he just looked like he thought I was hilarious.

When he went by that night I was outside with my father, who was home early for once. I told my father Sergei was following me, how he had this thing for me and wouldn't leave me alone. I was pretty sure he *did* have a thing for me, but I wanted to be completely sure. I wanted his complete attention.

My father signalled to him to stop. He started blasting him. Sergei looked at him and said, "I live down the road, dude. You can't tell me what to do." Then Sergei drove away really fast. My father was so pissed at Sergei and at me. It was so funny. But how was I supposed to know Sergei lived on our road? Later, when they questioned him, my father told the police how Sergei was obsessed with me. He didn't tell them how it really happened, how Sergei was just going to his house. They didn't need that fact.

AT SCHOOL THE NEXT day Sergei came up to me. "Isabella," he said, "I think you're trouble."

"Oh, I'm trouble, am I?" I smiled and tossed my hair back. I had this new stuff in it which enhanced the curl.

He shook his head and smiled back. "Why did you tell your father I was stalking you?"

"Well, I thought you were. I never saw you on our road before."

Then he started laughing again. "It's not *your* road. We've been living on the Brow of Mountain Road since way before you moved there. It's kind of sexy, your tunnel vision. The way you revolve around yourself like you are the sun and the moon," Sergei said. He started laughing again. He has these big soft lips and chocolate-cake eyes.

"Want me to come visit sometime when Daddy's away?" He leaned toward me and I could smell his warm skin.

"See, you are stalking me," I said, and I gave him the little smile I do in the mirror at home.

"Everyone wanted to know who was building that big-ass house. What was it, like, five years ago? You were just a little girl then." He smiled with those red lips. "Are you all grown-up now?"

"Wouldn't you like to know," I said in a soft little voice. I gave Sergei a wink and then walked away, saying, "See you around sometime." The kind of voice my mother used to use on my father when I was in bed and they didn't think I could hear. They put the back deck too close to my room. I'd never make that sort of mistake. I'd put my kids' rooms in the basement so they couldn't hear anything.

After my mother left, I told my father I wanted to have the guest room as my room, at the front of the house on the ground level. It was supposed to be a sitting room, but they didn't need it so it became this extra guest room and no one used it. He didn't care. We had the room all done up and he got me a new canopy bed. I've got an amazing bedroom. We used Cinderella Pink on the walls. Pink is the colour of pure love. The ceiling is Iced Violet. It's supposed to be calming. Sergei told me in Russia it's the colour of the dead.

WHEN MY MOTHER LEFT and my dad brought in Bewitching Interiors he let me make all the choices. He trusted me. *You have an eye for detail. You are all about the detail.* It's true. I am all about the detail, the trim, the edge, the look. The first thing I'd do in this stupid jail—sorry, *youth centre*—is put some colour on the walls. How can they expect these young people to make any changes in their lives with such dingy colours?

The interior designer brought all these paint swatches and took me to a special flooring store to pick out carpet. She wore silk skirts that swished and I'm pretty sure her feet didn't touch the ground when she walked. There was a way she had when she looked at me, with this little smile, as though she knew I understood how beyond the drab dull world I was stuck in, behind it, was a realm of raging colour and enchantment where people like she and I belonged.

We picked out spectacular fabric to have the furniture reupholstered in. It was really gorgeous, just perfect. Every day when I'd come home from school one more part of the house would be finished. It looked like a new house. My father loved it. It was like we were papering right over my mother, painting her out of the picture.

MY FATHER HAS FINALLY lifted his head and he wants to talk about Sergei. But I don't want to talk about him, to have his putrid name on my lips.

I remember when I finally let Sergei drive me home from school. I was always the only one who got off the bus at my stop and no one was ever waiting for me. This would make some girls nervous but not me. But the day before Sergei drove me home, there was a noise in the woods when I got off the bus and it did creep me out a bit. Maybe it was reporters or something, trying to get dirt on my father. I went inside and peeked out the window but nothing came out of the woods.

The next day I got Sergei to drive me home from school, just in case. My father was never home after school so I wasn't worried about him walking in. And sure enough, just when we got in the door my phone rang and it was my father: he had a meeting so he'd be home late, I should microwave something for my dinner.

Sleep tight, goodnight, goodnight, goodnight.

We went out on the deck looking out over the Valley. He took out a joint. "You smoke?" I just shrugged and giggled. He lit up and then showed me how. He didn't even laugh when I coughed, just patted me on the back and helped me take another toke. "You don't always get high the first time," he said. But next thing I knew my head was as light as sparkles and I was twirling around. I was wearing red shoes and he kept calling me Dorothy.

It was spring and I could hear these evening birds and I took him by the hand into my canopy bed. He was so heavy and he said he didn't want to hurt me and then I couldn't stop laughing. "It's not the first time for everything, you asshole," I said, slapping him on the back. He was surprised, and it was the funniest thing I ever saw. That's what I loved about being high, laughing my ass off.

"Come on, Russian," I said.

"Dorothy," he said, looking into my eyes. "Aren't you a bad girl."

"I'm not Dorothy," I told him. "I'm the Wicked Witch of the West."

"YOU'RE FIERCE," HE WHISPERED with a huge smile the next day when he saw me at school. "My wicked witch." I winked at him and he smiled.

I didn't bother telling Sergei that when I was little I saw a real witch who I was related to. Just after we built the house, I was on the front lawn with my parents. They were deciding whether to hire a new landscaping service. Then an old woman with frizzy hair on a horse and wagon came out of a little trail in the woods across the road. She stopped right in front of the house and gave us the evil eye. My mother ran over to talk to her. My father didn't go anywhere near that shrivelled old lunatic who kept waving her arms at me and yelling "corruption, beware," and stuff like that.

My father whispered it was my mother's distant cousin who lived alone on the north side of the

Mountain near the bay in an old house on the Flying Squirrel Road. Poor old Lucretia had troubles, he said. She had been in jail for a long time. It was the bad side of the family. It was a pity, he said. But even as a kid I knew he didn't care about a crazy old person. My mother was wringing her hands together. The old lady went *bumpity bump* away over the road, staring at me the whole time. What a freaky bitch. I wasn't scared of her and stuck out my tongue when my parents turned away. I knew she was a witch of some kind. A real witch.

We had this great thing all year, Sergei coming over and him doing whatever chores my father wanted done, and getting high and having sex in my bedroom until we were in the store and she came by, that girl. Lulu. What a stupid name. Sergei says it's short for Lucille. Nicknames are for freaks. No one has ever called me anything but Isabella. Once a teacher called me Izzy and I stared at her until I thought I had frozen her to ice. "Isabella," I said. "We don't shorten it. Ever." The teacher bit her lip. She never called me anything else again.

LULU AND SERGEI NEVER really went out, he said. He just really liked her but it was a couple of years ago. He had to do community service work at the senior citizens' home as a part of his sentence for some crime he committed when he was fifteen, and she volunteered there, taking the old drooling people out for a bit of fresh air. He had to work in the gardens and so she'd go by pushing some old vegetable in a wheelchair, I bet winking her stupid eye at him while he killed all those weeds.

But her name kept coming up all the time after we saw her in the store. For five months it was like she was always with us. We went to a movie and when we were buying popcorn the guy at the popcorn counter asked Sergei if I was his sister. And then he asked if Sergei had seen Lulu lately, said how Lulu was so hot and he couldn't believe he let her get away. That guy was lucky I didn't come around the counter and stick his face in the boiling hot buttery topping, because nothing would have made me happier than seeing his skin blister and melt. I was so pissed I walked out of the theatre and threw my popcorn all over the parking lot. Sergei tried telling me the guy was just an idiot, and he was jealous because my father was a rich politician.

Once I went with him when he was buying groceries for his grandmother and there Lulu was at the end of the aisle, all little and cute, waving at him like she was sitting on a float in a dumb parade. I wanted to bash her head in with a can of peaches. And Sergei's grandmother, she just loved Lulu, asking about her whenever I was there, like she was disappointed every time I came in the door. She even called me Lulu once. I almost lost it, but Sergei corrected her and told her I was Isabella. Oh yes, she said, but I could tell from her voice she was let down, like she was hoping if she counted to three I'd transform into that stupid Lulu.

"I thought you said you never went out with her," I asked him. "So how does your grandmother know who she is?"

Sergei said he drove his grandmother to some social club for old people at the nursing home, and Lulu would do crafts with them sometimes or read to them. He said she played the flute and would do little concerts.

Lulu, Lulu, tweeting away on her flute, like some bird that won't shut up. She was just doing whatever she could to get Sergei back—and he was defending her.

I couldn't stop thinking about her, asking him about her. I told him I wasn't going to have sex with him anymore, how it was over unless he got rid of her. I just wanted him to tell her to leave us alone. To take a stand. I wanted her out of our lives. Sergei kept saying she wasn't a problem, I should just forget about her. Well, how was I supposed to do that with her popping up everywhere we went? How, I asked him, was I supposed to believe him? How was he going to prove she wasn't a problem?

I told Sergei that if he didn't get her to stop bugging me I'd tell my father he'd been coming over every night for months, and I'd tell the police he was a drug dealer. And no more touching my body. No more Wicked Witch of the West ever again, just Dorothy, and Dorothy isn't any fun. He kept saying it was all in my mind, that I was getting totally paranoid and neurotic. Our town was so small we were bound to run into her sometimes, he said. She wasn't stalking him and he wasn't lying or hiding anything. But I could tell. I just have this extra sense. I'm not like other people.

IT WAS THE WINKING. If only she hadn't winked. Winking was *our* thing, I told Sergei when we drove home from the store. "Some things are supposed to be sacred!" I yelled at him. I couldn't get to sleep at night. I'd see her with her long hair and those big blue eyes, her sexy smile, those long lashes like feathers touching as she winked right in front of me. And that's when I told him he had to get rid of her.

"Well, I guess he took you literally," my father said when I first told him this. I nodded. Yes, this was what happened. Sergei took it literally.

I told my father and the police about the evening it happened. Sergei had said we should go out, he wanted to take me out and show me something special. If I'd just come with him, he said, it would all be better.

I wanted to believe him. It was getting dark later now because it was June. It was a pretty evening. The colours were gorgeous, all these different shades of purple and blue, just like eye shadow.

Sergei drove me to the woods near this pond where he said there were water lilies blooming. He was going to show me a surprise, prove his love to me. He was already high when he picked me up. He was on meth. That's not something I did. He's the drug addict.

We sat in his car and smoked a joint and then walked in on this path through the trees. It was like being in a storybook. And then we came out to this beautiful clearing and the sunset was reflecting in the pond, like the water was magic. There was a snap and I looked up and who was there but her. She must have followed us. Lulu. The sun hit her hair and she was standing there with the deep-green forest behind her like fucking Snow White. She took a few steps forward and smiled, all nervous, and said, "What was so important you needed to talk to me about, Sergei?"

Then Sergei got crazy. "Are you following me?" he said. "I told you to leave me alone. I love Isabella, not you. Can't you accept that?"

"But Sergei, you told me to meet you here," she said. I told the police what Lulu said. And she started crying. "But I love you," she said to Sergei. I'm sure she said that. It sounded like that. It made me so mad.

It happened so fast. He went up to her and grabbed her by her long hair and she fell down on her knees.

And then Sergei kicked her in the side and Lulu bent over. She couldn't catch her breath. I was frozen at first. "See," he said to me, "I'm showing you." He kicked her in the eye, her winking eye.

I was crying, saying he should stop. That's what I was doing. My hands are sweating, remembering this.

"Don't hurt her," I screamed. "I won't tell my dad you've been coming over. I won't tell him about the drugs. I was just kidding," I screamed.

But he was out of control. When she tried to get up he came behind her. She was on her knees. He came behind her and put out his hands, really slowly. She wasn't moving fast so he wasn't rushing. He held out his hands like he was going to put them under her arms and help her get up. But then he moved really quickly and put them around her neck and started to squeeze. She started wiggling, thrashing around, making these horrible sounds. I can hear them now, these little gurgles, gasping for breath, and he squeezed even harder. She had on a fine gold necklace and it wrapped all around his finger so tight it cut right into him but he just kept going. Violence takes the pain away. The necklace wasn't on her neck when they pulled her out of the pond. The police never mentioned it—it must have fallen off into the water. It's a deep pond. I grabbed his arm to get him to stop, and that's when he spun around and hit me in the face and I fell down.

I STARTED CRYING WHEN I told my father this when he first came in with all his stubble. I cried when I told the police and my lawyer, every time I've told them. My nose was running, snot all over my face, all over my bruised cheek. Crying is disgusting. The youth worker who came in to check if everything was okay was this really cute guy and I didn't want him to see me looking like a blubbering mess. After he left, my father reached across the table and put his hand on my shoulder. "It's okay, Isabella," he said. "We'll get through this. This is my fault for not being around more . . . I'm so sorry." His voice broke and I took my hands down from my face so he could see me, my eyes red and blotchy. There were tears running down his cheeks as he held my hand.

MY FATHER ISN'T CRYING now. He just yawns and I can smell his disgusting breath. Too much coffee. He hasn't even had time to whiten his teeth. He just waits for me to say something but I've said all there is to say and so for this visit, he'll just have to sit there and learn this.

After my mother left I used to wonder what she would have looked like if the brakes hadn't worked on her car, what her face would have looked like if it had smashed through the windshield, glass stuck in her big sparkling eyes.

For the last year when my mother called for our

Sunday talk, I didn't bother answering the phone. She finally called my father at work. He told me I should really find time to take her call. I just shrugged and said I'd see what I could do. He sighed. "Isabella, when your mind is made up it's like trying to stir dried concrete." I thought that was stupid because concrete is so ugly, and I felt like kicking him.

But here I am, surrounded by concrete. I told the warden how ugly this place is and it was the one time he laughed. "Why would we want to pretend you're somewhere pleasant?" he asked me. "This isn't a boarding school, Isabella. This isn't a hotel. Or some storybook palace. You need to grow up and take responsibility for yourself."

I would have liked to shove chopsticks in his temples, nice and slow, right into his brain.

"Whatever," I said.

MY FATHER FINALLY STANDS up and his chair shrieks as it rubs against the floor. It's such an ugly sound and I put my hands over my ears. My father pats me on the head and he leaves the room. He probably wants me to ask him for help but I won't be brought down to that level. I already told him what happened.

SERGEI AND I WERE standing by the pond and Lulu was lying there, dead. I was hyperventilating. Then Sergei came over to me and started to kiss me. He was crazy, all pumped up on drugs and from the adrenaline. It surges through your body. I was still really stoned and I felt dizzy. When we first got there and parked, he took out this joint and we smoked it. It made my lungs burn. I don't know what he had in it, but there was a funny taste in my mouth, and I could feel my heart go faster, like every hair on my body was standing up a bit, like my skin could feel every single bit of the wind, the warmth of the sun, like it was all magnified and it was like I was ten feet tall except my head felt like a balloon that was going to float up and away any second. And then it was like I was floating outside of myself, darting all around, a dragonfly, watching myself as we walked to the pond.

And then it all happened and we were there with her at our feet. My heart was pounding and I was dripping sweat. I pushed him away and we stood there looking at each other. A frog croaked from the water and we both looked at the pond. And then she started moaning. She wasn't dead. I couldn't believe it, with all those kicks, being strangled like that, and still alive. I told Sergei he had to stop, how he couldn't cross that final line. Just a kick to her head, he said. That's all it will take." She sort of crawled, but she went the wrong way, toward the pond. She got up and was wobbling. And then Sergei walked over and gave her a push with his foot and she fell in. That's all it took, a little tap. I would have jumped in to save her but the pond looked really deep. She didn't struggle much, just floated there, face down among the water lilies with the sun setting on her long hair.

And then those bird-watching people came hiking out of the woods. They had a cellphone and called the police. I was at the edge of the pond holding a big stick when they saw me. I was only trying to drag her to land. They backed up like they thought I was going to hit them with it. Sergei ran away into the trees and I followed him. It was dark with all the leaves overhead. He lit a cigarette. I told him he'd have to take responsibility. It was then that he said he would tell the truth, he would make sure they knew it was him. I ran back out crying, asking the nature people to help me while the Lulu bird floated in the water and Sergei ran away to his car.

I CAN HEAR THEM coming down the hall now.

The door opens and the sheriff is standing there with cuffs and shackles. "Time to go for a ride," he says, no smile. "Stand up, please and put your hands behind your back."

I stand up and face the ugly beige wall. It seems to move forward, closing in on me, challenging me. I won't close my eyes and give in.

I was looking at this same wall the first time I talked to my lawyer. He was telling me that the police were interviewing Sergei for the millionth time, and if the judge accepted Sergei's testimony, they'd drop the charges against me when I came to court to enter a plea.

The metal snaps together as they put the cuffs on. They don't say anything about my sweating hands. The shackles take longer. I'm just standing there, being cooperative. The shackles catch on the leg of my grey sweatpants. The sheriff apologizes to me.

"It's okay," I say, looking at the wall.

And just then, the warden comes in. He clears his throat, that's how I know it's him. "Your lawyer just called. Your friend Sergei is going to testify," he says.

I just smirk. *Tell me something I don't know*, I think.

But then he does. "The Russian says that you killed the girl. He couldn't go through with it so you did it and he hit you, he tried to stop you," he says in his flat voice. "It's true, isn't it?"

I don't say a word.

Instead, I smile.

Smile at the beige wall. You know that kind of smile, the smile of a thousand knives. The wall trembles.

"They dredged the pond and found the necklace."

The warden clears his throat again. "They are charging you with murder in the first degree."

I keep right on smiling because I'm going to stick a knife in Sergei's gut as soon as I get my hands on him, and I can't wait to see his face then. I should have known he wouldn't keep his word. You can't trust Russians. No one will ever believe him. No one will take his word over mine. Or my father's. My father is with me every step of the way. If there's one thing I can count on, it's that.

I'll see Sergei at the courthouse. I'll make him feel pain like he has never felt pain before, and he'll be afraid to even think my name for the rest of his pathetic life.

I remember my father's face the very first time I saw him in this place, the morning after Lulu died. He was so tired. He closed his eyes and then opened them—and then he opened them wider as he looked at my hand on the table. He reached out and ran his pen along the inside of my index finger where there was a deep cut like a red thread running from the bottom of my finger to the top. "Where did you get that cut, Isabella?" he asked, his voice almost a whisper. I looked at him then just like I'm looking at the warden now—with eyes reflecting back the beige.

THE DIPLOMAT

THE DIPLOMAT

WIEDERVEREINIGUNG, the German teacher said. Viola knew the Chinese student named Henry would translate just as he had since starting the class two weeks ago, always trying to help, but she already knew this word. It was impossible to be in Germany in 1995 and not know. The teacher, a plump middle-aged woman, told them the fourth anniversary was approaching, and she went around the circle and made them repeat, stretching their lips, raising their eyebrows, as though they were warming up for an opera.

"*Wie-der-ver-ei-ni-gung.*"

"This means reunification," Henry said, looking at Viola from across the table. In perfect English. With an accent just like hers. She blushed. His smile was small and careful.

"I know what it means," she replied in halting

German, her eyes closing. The Berlin Wall had come down four years earlier.

"Die Berliner Mauer," Viola said slowly.

Apparently Henry interpreted this as confusion. "The wall," he said in his remarkable English, as though he'd grown up down the road from her. "The Berlin Wall." He stretched his arms out as though showing her how big it was, in case she thought it was a fence for goats like the one on the small saltwater farm on Campobello Island in the Bay of Fundy, near her parents' house, the farm where Ben now was...without her. The teacher clucked and reminded them to speak German. Henry smiled at Viola again, and Mary from Australia giggled as though they were all still teenagers.

It was a small class in a small language school in the centre of Frankfurt, *im Zentrum*, as the Germans said. Viola had been in the German class for three months. She took the train in every weekday from the small town she lived in with Ralf, whom she'd met on a trip she'd taken to Vietnam after finishing her history degree. When she spoke German at home Ralf would stroke her hair and say: "You are like a kitchen appliance, macerating every syllable. It's very cute, *Schatzie*. You sound like a Turk."

The director had brought in the new Chinese students on Monday morning. The director was an old German hippie, always winking and telling Viola to eat muesli. Mary said that during introductions, Henry had perked up immediately when Viola said she was from Campobello Island. Viola hadn't noticed — she often shut her eyes when she spoke German, and thought of home. It made her feel braver, to think of the good things back home. Henry was from Beijing. He had been in Frankfurt for one month. He was thirty-one years old.

Every Monday they began with a new expression or word they had learned on the weekend. This class, Viola offered *Heimweh*. Henry nodded in agreement when Viola said she missed Canada.

"Homesick," he said, as though he could picture the sea urchins and shells she saw behind her eyelids. Viola squinted, thinking his name couldn't actually be Henry. It wasn't Chinese. He told her later it was a name he had taken for Westerners. His real name was Sun He Peng.

On coffee break Henry was talking with the other two Chinese men as she walked by. Henry smiled and looked down at his feet and then back at her. He was tall. He'd laughed later when she said she thought Chinese men were all short. He told her he used to think Caucasians wore sunglasses so their eyes wouldn't change colour in the sun. "I didn't know the colour of your eyes at first," he said. "Your eyes were always closed when you were speaking. They are green like the ocean."

Henry had worked at the Canadian embassy in Beijing. He also had worked at the Chinese embassy in Ottawa for one year, part of his training. He'd perfected his English there.

"A translator?" Viola asked.

"A diplomat. At first I thought you didn't understand the language. You are just shy. Forgive me."

Viola laughed and closed her eyes and her cheeks were hot.

AFTER THE MONDAY CLASS when the Chinese students arrived, Mary had proclaimed them a mini-UN. Mary was an accountant from Sydney and she was living here with her fiancé, Helmut, a banker she'd met at a conference. He had a telescope. He loved the night sky. They were going to Australia soon to get married. They would go to the desert for their honeymoon so Helmut could see the night sky without *light pollution*. Viola had never heard this term before.

There was a young couple from Turkey, *Gastarbeiter*, guest workers doing industrial work there weren't enough Germans for. Sixteen-year-old Farzad from Tehran who mourned the fall of the Shah and with his large aqua eyes followed every move of Kwan-Sun, seventeen and from Korea, a nanny for a wealthy German family. Padma was from Bombay, her husband an English investment banker. It was the second time they'd been married to each other and she anticipated another divorce and possibly a third marriage. They were made for each other, she said, but only incrementally. It was Padma who said the Chinese were refugees. "The riots, you know, the massacre, in 1989," she whispered.

And there was Lucien from Burkina Faso, married to a German historian. He and his wife Helga spoke French together, he had told the class. They'd married in Ouagadougou, and now she had a position at the university in Frankfurt. Helga's last name was von Feldenburg. In the olden days *von* was a sign of nobility, Lucien stated.

Yes, their teacher agreed, but German nobility ended with the abolition of the monarchy in 1919.

"*Ja, ja,*" Lucien had said, leaning back in his chair, his eyes sparkling and his skin like espresso against the creamy white wall. "But abolition does not mean the old ideas disappear. *Ce n'est jamais si facile que ça, mes amis.*" He looked at the teacher and then at Viola and cocked his eyebrow.

"*Ja,*" she said, eyes closing, in her mind sitting with Ben on the back porch of his family farmhouse, which had come down through five generations to him. They ate chèvre with sun-dried tomatoes on homemade brown bread. *Don't go on this trip abroad*, Ben said, looking out over the beach, crying so quietly. *Stay here and marry me. We'll run your family inn and my mother's farm, do the summer market for the tourists, and go sailing on Saturday afternoons.* Viola had cried too but she did leave and had not returned.

HENRY WOULD ALWAYS COME to the park after class with the other students and they scattered to benches under the gloomy November clouds. Henry often sat by the fountain with Viola and asked her about Canada. At first she was reluctant to discuss where she had come from, but he was easy to talk with and every time they sat together she shared more and more. Viola wasn't used to anyone but Ben having such interest in her. She told Henry she was living with Ralf, how they'd met in Saigon where Viola had moved after graduating from university with what Ralf called a useless arts degree. She had begged Ben to come with her but he said he already had a life on Campobello, commitments and responsibilities he couldn't leave.

Viola's only friend in Saigon was her roommate, Evangeline. They shared a tiny apartment and taught ESL at the same small school. She was a girl from Nova Scotia who made friends easily and, like Henry, spent most of her time asking questions and listening. She insisted on brushing her teeth with the tap water so she could get used to the local bacteria and as a result she had constant diarrhea. She said adventure was not all it was cracked up to be and they should both go home. But Viola wasn't ready for that. She helped Evangeline pack and went with her to the airport where Evangeline gave her a small silver necklace with a delicate starfish hanging from the chain. Evangeline said it was a good luck charm for travellers that her father had given to her, but she didn't need it as much as Viola would. Viola cried when Evangeline went through the gate. It wasn't long after that she agreed to come to Germany with Ralf, rather than scurry back to the island in New Brunswick, embarrassed she had left in the first place.

After a month of their bench chats, Viola blurted out to Henry how she'd left Campobello because she wanted adventure, a journey which wasn't halted by land's end. She had never shared anything like this with Ralf. Viola knew he would roll his eyes. He was impatient with what he called inconsequential conversation. But Henry was the opposite and Viola couldn't help herself. She told him about Ben and how she wept when she said she couldn't marry him. She was too young. She didn't know what she wanted to do with her life.

"Yes, sometimes when we have too much choice it's hard to make even one," Henry said.

"That's exactly how it is for me, Henry. But Ben always knew what he wanted. He never felt like the water encircling Campobello Island was going to drown him, the way I did. Ben always said the ocean simply meant there was an enormous world beyond and it made him appreciate the world he was actually living in. Ben has always blamed his father's death on his need to see the world. So I understand why Ben is content at home."

But her voice had caught then and Henry tilted his beautiful head to the side, knowing there were some things she couldn't speak of easily. It had broken Viola's heart to leave Ben behind but it would have broken her spirit to stay. It was easier to at least try to forget Campobello Island and everyone on it.

Henry asked about Viola's boyfriend, Ralf, who was a software engineer. He'd been married once before and had a twenty-three-year-old daughter, the same age as Viola. She lived in New York and would call sometimes, usually hanging up if Viola answered. *I don't recognize you*, the daughter said once. *You are just one more. Don't think you are the only one even now.* Ralf said his daughter was jealous. She was insecure. She refused to grow up. Ralf did research on how to use the internet to make telephone calls. It was the way of the future, he said. He travelled frequently, so Viola was studying German, something to keep her busy while he was gone. She had no work papers, no official status. "I might have to fly back to Canada if we don't sort something out. Ralf wants to get married but that seems so final."

Henry's face relaxed into what seemed to Viola to be a look of solace. "It might be a good idea to go home, Viola. There are worse places to live. I have a great affinity for Canadians. They've been kind to me."

"That might be the case for you, but Canadians aren't as nice as everyone seems to think. It's easy to be a coward underneath all that beer and bacon." Viola told him the Canadian embassy in Saigon had closed up shop in the night and fled just before Saigon fell to the North Vietnamese in 1975. The Vietnamese who'd worked for the Canadians found an abandoned building in the morning. "That wasn't very compassionate," she said, looking at the sky.

Henry's voice was serious, what Viola imagined it would sound like if he were addressing a group of students. "Viola, no one puts their best foot forward when the army is advancing. Things did not go as Ho Chi Minh planned. He was hopeful after the Battle of Dien Bien Phu in the First Indochina War. But the negotiations at the Geneva Conference in 1954 were not what Ho wanted. Zhou Enlai was the Chinese diplomat involved in these negotiations, assisting the Vietminh. Zhou Enlai was brilliant."

"Is he why you became a diplomat?"

Henry laughed. "Oh, Viola, I was selected and told I would be a diplomat and that, like Zhou Enlai, my job would be to think of my people. You know, nearly a quarter million Chinese died in what you call the Korean War."

"I can't imagine so many people," Viola said.

He closed his eyes. "Zhou's main concern was keeping the Americans away. A permanent partition of the Vietnamese peninsula suited China." Henry paused and then opened his eyes and looked at the pigeons. "The freedom of my people suited me."

Viola slapped a small puddle with her shoe.

Henry looked at her foot and then at her face. "We have a saying: *The general sees with only one eye, the diplomat with both.* War may be the domain of soldiers, but resolutions are always the purview of diplomats." Henry smiled. "Uncle Ho discovered even hope must be negotiated. But Vietnam was his home and he would not abandon it after he had returned from so many years in exile."

Viola made tiny ripples in the small puddle with the toe of her shoe. "Ben's father was an American photo-journalist and now he's buried on Campobello Island. He was a combat photographer and died on a helicopter shot down near Danang. He was twenty-nine when he died and Ben was just a baby. Ben puts flowers on his father's grave every Sunday afternoon even when it's snowing. He'll never know his dad, but he tries at the grave. He really believes by staying on Campobello Island he can somehow be close to him and have the life his father threw away. Ben won't leave the island, not even for me." Viola squeezed her eyes shut to keep the tears in but they dripped down her cheeks anyway.

Henry took her hand. "I understand your Ben. In China we pray to our ancestors. The old ways are slow to pass. My father was sad when I went to Beijing. He said to complete the circle of life one must bury one's father. I laughed at him, Viola, but I laughed less as I grew older. It is our history with the people we love which binds us together. Being close to the graves of the dead has life in it even if you cannot see this." He took out a tissue and dabbed her eyes and cheeks, and kept holding her hand.

She moved closer to him and he put his arm around her. "Ben puts silk flowers on the grave in the winter, not real ones because they'd freeze. I wasn't very diplomatic when I said I wouldn't marry him, how I left the island so fast." She could feel the warmth of his leg next to hers. They both laughed and Viola felt warm then. She rested her head on Henry's shoulder and his voice was very quiet as he leaned toward her and whispered with his lips on her ear, "Regret is never worth the price, Viola. We pay for the rest of our lives." They

sat together without speaking for another fifteen minutes. When they walked to the subway a large flock of
pigeons at the other end of the park lifted up into the
grey sky.

ON MOST FRIDAY AFTERNOONS some of the students
ate lunch at a cheap Yugoslavian restaurant near the
school. Henry was the only Chinese student who ever
joined them. After, they would walk together to the
subway, the U-Bahn. It was always Mary, Viola, and
Farzad who would walk together, but these days Farzad
and Kwan-Sun had been walking in the other direction,
holding hands.

Henry began to wait and walk with Mary and Viola.
He and Mary would board the train on the left and Viola
would take the one on the right to the Hauptbahnhof,
the main train station, and then take the S-Bahn com-
muter train to Darmstadt, back to the empty apartment.
Ralf would be home on the weekends and they'd eat
and then ride his motorcycle through the countryside.
He knew she was homesick and hoped the adventures
would cure her. He would take her to medieval castles
in the hills and as they'd climb the turrets he'd tousle
her hair and tell her she was gorgeous.

Ralf never approved of her housekeeping. He'd
unpack his suitcase and then vacuum. It wasn't a

criticism; it was how he relaxed. You had to stay on top of the dust, he'd comment. And then he'd tie her to the bed and take a feather duster to her, from her toes, up her legs, over her breasts, her face, feathers soft on her eyelashes. And he'd pack again on a Sunday evening, gone before she awoke, alone.

THE DAY SHE WENT back to Henry's apartment they'd been swarmed by an army of pigeons in the park. They had gone back to the park after lunch, just the two of them. The pigeons of Frankfurt were nasty and knew no discretion. They didn't wait quietly for crumbs but hopped and leapt about in a frenzy, even the maimed birds, things with one eye, one leg, bald heads.

She wondered how they got their injuries and Henry laughed. "What is significant is how they survive them." He joked they were ancestors of war birds—while the bomb-flattened *Zentrum* of Frankfurt might be nothing more than a replica, the pigeons carried the DNA of the survivors. They could withstand an apocalypse now. There were pigeons in China, he told her. But having pets was now considered bourgeois. "They are not in the parks like this," he said.

Henry always wanted more stories of Campobello Island, and she told him it was near Maine, near Passamaquoddy Bay—it was easy to talk about the

geography. Her hands fluttered in front of her face, in ·
front of her breasts, up over her head, as she drew him
a map in the air. She told him of Ben and the goats,
and the summer market where they worked together.
"He thinks if his father had been a farmer and not a
combat photographer, he wouldn't have died. I went
away to university, but I came home every holiday,
every summer. The autumn after I graduated I went
to Saigon. I went because I saw his father's photos.
They spoke to me. Ben said I'd never come back. And
I haven't. The island felt as though it was growing
smaller every day."

Viola asked Henry why he was in Frankfurt. He
was so easy to talk to and yet shared so little. He'd
been at Tiananmen Square, he told her—still watching the pigeons, his voice matter-of-fact. He'd been in
prison and then under house arrest. The Canadians
had negotiated on his behalf, for his safety. His voice
became faint and she bent close. His father had died
during this time.

"Could you ever go back?" Viola asked, holding her
arms up as she shook her cold hands.

Henry's eyes followed her fingers as though they
were wings in the sky, and he reached for them, clasp-
ing her icy hands in his as he told her no, he did not
foresee it. "Nothing yet in the tea leaves," he said,
grinning.

Henry wanted to know again about Campobello and she told him of the beaches, of Franklin D. Roosevelt's summer place which was now part of a park. Viola's family home was now an inn. Her father was ill. He had frontal lobe dementia, something Viola never knew existed until the doctor called a family meeting. He would have to be institutionalized. It was only a matter of time, her mother had written in a letter. It was easier to be away, Viola said.

"It is nice you have a choice, Viola."

She closed her eyes then, but there was no judgment in Henry's voice and he held her hand tighter.

It was now late in the afternoon and they got up and walked toward the subway. Viola asked about the camp he was staying in. Henry let out a big guffaw sort of laugh, which was unlike him. He never let out more than a quiet chuckle. When he regained his composure, he told Viola his accommodations were not actually in a refugee camp. It was not what she saw in the news—the tents and jeeps, aid workers doling out bowls of rice. Viola's naïveté was endlessly amusing to him, and to Viola herself. "Housing is perhaps a better word than camp." He said her island view of the world was charming.

They had not discussed how Viola would come home with him. This week Ralf was away in Poland until Saturday evening. They rode the train together and both stood up as it slowed at Henry's stop. The door had slid open and he held out his hand.

It was a tall, generic building. Henry and the two other Chinese classmates shared the small, tidy apartment. Two bedrooms, with one of them sleeping in the living room. The roommates had not been in class—away for the weekend, Henry said. Viola did not ask where.

Henry led her by the hand to a little bedroom with a mattress on the floor and a tiny table beside the bed, on it a photo of a smiling young Chinese woman holding a baby, and beside it, a black-and-white picture of a young boy and his father and mother, standing by a cow.

Henry turned to Viola and took her face between his hands and kissed her, sucking her breath inside of him, her fingers all over his flesh, mapping her way to him. They made love on the thin mattress, his long hard body pressed down and in on hers, spreading over her as the shadow from a tree would. Henry was silent and when she cried out he covered her lips with his mouth.

He asked her, after, as they lay there drinking tea, if she would stay and marry Ralf. Or if she would go home to her young man with the flowers. Frankfurt was not a city for her, he whispered. There were no beaches. "As the Germans say, *Zu Hause ist es doch am schönsten*," he said with a smile. The late-afternoon sun tunnelled in through the small window. "No place like home," he said.

Henry told Viola they'd said his wife and daughter would be safe, but only on the condition he go into exile without them. It was the Canadian embassy that had arranged things with Germany. Henry hoped he could one day go to Canada. They were working on this possibility, but it would be years, and his life was in exile now, he knew this. There would be no visits to his father's grave.

Henry cooked noodles for supper and early the next morning he brought her persimmons and tea. Grey sky filled the window and she imagined she was on the shores of Campobello, the traffic outside the surf breaking on the sand-and-pebble beach. Henry touched the necklace that draped over her collar bones, the tiny silver starfish perched near her shoulder. He straightened it as Viola held up her hand and spread her fingers out. "Did you know the starfish is a symbol for safe travel?" Viola asked.

She thought of Ben and his goats, and his armful of wildflowers for his father on Sundays in July, her father now drooling in a wheelchair, his quivering fingers and small, grateful smile when she took his rough hand in hers, conversation an incomprehensible clamour to him but finding reassurance in this touch—as though Viola was still a little girl and they were sitting on the dock together while he mended his lobster traps.

Viola remembered running on the beach with Ben

when the evening sky hung before them in muted oranges and banners of crimson clouds. A hot afternoon in the boat and the wind snapping the sail with that crack she loved so much. The sun rising on the Bay of Fundy, delicate solar yellows staining the glassy waves on a June morning as salt-spray roses bloomed at the top of the beach. The quiet of dawn, a quiet Viola realized she carried with her wherever she went, a solitude in which she carried Ben and her father. This was Henry's gift of perspective, a restoration and appreciation of the past which had been so brutally cut away from him.

"Viola," Henry whispered, taking her hand in his, "home is something we must sometimes negotiate. But it is always worth the negotiations, no matter how complex. You must not send yourself into exile when you can return and make your way. We Chinese have a saying: *Your heart will lead you to a path and if you do not follow it, you will find, as the years pass, that you are still at its beginning.*" It was then he glanced at the photo on the small table. He shut his eyes and was quiet for a moment before he took Viola's hand and kissed the palm, his lips soft and warm on her cold, pale skin.

FULL BLEED

It will be a descent through the darkness of the familiar
into the world where, like the blind man cured in the
gospels, he sees men as if they were trees, but walking.
This is the beginning of vision...

— FLANNERY O'CONNOR, *Mystery and Manners*

ADAM HAS NO IDEA why he agreed to take his ancient
in-laws on this stupid outing over dirt roads through the
Valley and up into the distant hills they call mountains.
He feels like he's changing into someone else, reckless,
with no appreciation for caution. They've been driving for an hour on tiny roads that make Adam think
of another time, of early settler days. Adam is from
Vancouver and hates rural life on the East Coast. There's
too much wild nature here. Big trees in city parks with
groomed, accessible paths are more to his liking.

Still, he picked up Grandma Charlotte and Great
Aunt Doris-the-Spinster after lunch, for a drive in the
country. As soon as the women got in the car, though,
Charlotte insisted that they visit the site of the old
abandoned homestead. She had no interest in his little
Sunday drive to see the autumn foliage. "I'm no tourist,
Adam, not like you," Charlotte said.

But Aunt Doris didn't want to do the trip to the homestead this year, she said, and why was Charlotte insisting they go today? They usually went much earlier in the season, she reminded her, when it wasn't almost dark in the late afternoon. "And besides, I'm done with going up the Mountain to keep the family memories alive, Charlotte. We're old now and the past is past. You agreed we'd be normal old ladies for once."

Charlotte began sobbing and Doris finally agreed just to get her to be quiet. Doris had worked as a clerk in the town office until she retired and if ever asked about it, she said the job required a specialization in handling idiots. Charlotte clutched her purse and giggled, pleased as a conniving child, her tears gone as quickly as they had welled up. "Due north, Adam," she said.

Now Adam is driving north toward the Mountain and he has a choice to make. It's up to him to refuse to take them north to the homestead, decide not to take them anywhere after all, or to insist on just a short afternoon drive as originally planned. But, smiling like a fiend, Adam suddenly shouts "Yes!"

He starts up the Mountain thinking of how his wife had always described the annual outing as taking the ladies on a *short little drive* to see the pretty leaves. She never once mentioned taking them to the ancestral place deep in the back country and he has no idea where on earth they are going. Charlotte is so sure of herself, though, that Adam assumes he can find it with her directions.

As they reach the top of the mountain there is a bad omen of a house, a decaying Victorian with an enormous rotting verandah and boarded-up windows.

"Right there is where your wife's childhood best friend lived. Seraphina was her name. She was the one who put the idea of going to university into Bethie's head," Doris says in a clipped, sombre voice as she waves toward the house. "No one lives there now. That's what happens when you learn more than you need to." They continue on for another forty-five minutes. There is not another house in sight, just thick forest on either side of the small country road.

As the car bumps over the deep potholes Adam clings to the steering wheel, wondering why his wife might have lied about where exactly she took the old ladies every year. A part of Adam thinks he should turn around immediately. It is too late in the day for a long outing. It will get dark soon. The old ladies aren't dressed for a walk. They should go home. The old sensible Adam would do this. But the new Adam keeps driving.

He is a graphic designer turned publisher of graphic novels, everything unfolding in his mind in carefully structured grids and panels. All his days storyboarded. As they drive along the dirt road with dense forest on either side, Adam observes how the autumn leaves are

Pantone colours and part of the grid. The forest floor is a swatch book. Those long branches are PMS 1375. That massive leaf PMS 032 and the tree to the left is a brilliant PMS 101.

He, Adam, in the driver's seat of the car, Great Aunt Doris beside him with her short PMS 877 hair and practical scarf, Grandma Charlotte in the back with her huge, dyed-mauve bouffant, PMS 2562, wearing a dress and scarf more suitable for a party than for a walk in the country. No speech bubbles today.

They are in the middle of nowhere. Grandma Charlotte lets out a huge rattling wheeze and it reminds him of Elizabeth on her death bed. The grid collapses. His memories, his impulsiveness, they are making it impossible to maintain order in his vision of the world. Ever since Elizabeth died, he's felt like inside there is a part of him he's never known, a part that opened its eyes when Elizabeth took her last breath.

Adam glances in the rear-view mirror and Charlotte smiles, a sly smile, her eyes glancing side to side. He always used to think of her as a sweet old lady, simpleminded but harmless, always wearing a dress. She gives him an innocent little wave.

Adam feels guilty for being suspicious of the elderly woman, but he has a bad feeling in his stomach. There is something behind the storyboard he doesn't want to face. With the grid falling apart and his ability to structure his time and order his thoughts unreliable, he feels vulnerable, like whatever is hiding might leap out and he wouldn't even see it coming.

"Turn here, Adam dear," Grandma Charlotte says. "Bethie knew the way. She was such a good girl. She understood we needed to pay our respects, keep our connection to the past."

Adam feels a rush of rage thinking of how his wife never told him the truth about this annual excursion. Shame pushes the rage down. He always thought Elizabeth was embarrassed by her rough country upbringing, which explained why she didn't talk about it. Until he met her family, Adam had never heard anyone call her Beth, let alone "Bethie." She said her friends called her Elizabeth but her family would never surrender her childhood nickname. At least she had a name which allowed for that multiplicity of identities, Elizabeth had joked. She was always joking. Adam is filled with longing for her, how easily she navigated change and uncertainty. At the same time it hits Adam that maybe Elizabeth didn't talk much about her childhood because she was protecting him from it, not hiding her embarrassment.

Grandma Charlotte taps Adam on the shoulder. "Pull over right here, dear," she says.

He jumps. He's been as lost in his thoughts as on the road.

"Stop right now, Adam, I said," Charlotte yells. "What are you, deaf?"

Adam slams on the brakes. Not seeing a turnoff, he pulls over to the side of the road, Charlotte looking through the rear window as though she is expecting someone to greet them. But there is only impenetrable forest. Adam doesn't see a driveway, a mailbox, or even a marker — nothing but coloured trees.

He follows the women out of the car, Charlotte continuing to insist this is the right spot. Doris parts the branches and, sure enough, there is a trail, which may once upon a time have been a road. Doris flaps her hand over her shoulder. "It's hard to believe if you walk just a few miles that way you'll come to the Bay of Fundy. You'd never even know it was there for all the woods in between."

The air smells brown-sugar sweet, the pale sun softly illuminating the last of the purple asters. He and Elizabeth had named their youngest daughter for those flowers, Elizabeth's favourite. Adam tries but fails to summon the Pantone for the blossoms. The paper-thin leaves on the tree branches rustle in the breeze — now just orange, red, and yellow to him. Some have fallen but many still cling to the branches, though it strikes him that it might be the other way around — trees clinging to their cover of leaves, hiding something behind the brilliant colours.

Aunt Doris surveys the path. "You could hardly sling a cat through here. Why did I let you talk me into coming, Charlotte? Just because you're upset about Herman."

"Doris, you're always so hard on him. That's what he says, how we never understood him. He's blaming me too, now, because of you." Charlotte sets off on the trail and Adam and Aunt Doris follow.

"When were you talking to Herman? He's still in jail, isn't he? Charlotte, did they let him out early?" Doris's voice vibrates with anger and apprehension. "At least it wasn't for murder this time. You think it would have taught him, but no, he's bad through and through."

Charlotte turns and shakes her fist at her sister. "I haven't laid eyes on Herman, Doris."

Aunt Doris lets out a sigh of relief, much to the irritation of her sister, who whacks the trail with her cane. "I don't blame Herman for hating you so much, Doris. You don't even care that today is his birthday. Even if I don't see him, I still remember his birthday. All the years are swooping back at me. Time goes so fast. When I was a little girl no one ever told me life would move so fast," Charlotte says as she rubs her hands together. She quiets her voice and continues in a conversational tone, "Why, my goodness, I should have worn more practical gloves. My gout is flaring up.

These gloves are so pretty, though, don't you think? I knit them out of angora. Adam, you're so kind to take us old girls on our favourite outing." She grins, as though the argument they've just had never happened.

There hasn't been any rain in weeks and the dry leaves crackle as Adam and the old ladies walk on the path which, it's now clear, had been a farm road decades ago. It threads through the woods, which are growing increasingly darker, the silver birches lining the path looming like wraiths. Adam looks at the sun: it's later than he thought. He should have planned better for this afternoon out, used his GPS. He doesn't even know where they are, and his phone doesn't work here in Dog Fuck Nowhere. Adam sits in front of a computer all day long, fiddling with InDesign and answering emails, and then racing to pick up his daughters from daycare. But it's Sunday afternoon and the girls are at the babysitter's.

It's been just over a year since Elizabeth died — this annual outing with her decrepit relatives is part of his inheritance from her. Though what he thought he was inheriting was just a normal country drive — not a pilgrimage into the remains of her family's dark story.

That story is a piece of family lore that Elizabeth had shared with him before they got married, before he had met her family for the first time. The ancestral home — the ruins of which this path is leading them to—had burned to the ground with the great-great-grandmother trapped inside. Elizabeth had told him the story as though it were a fairy tale, something for scaring children, nothing more. The same casual way she had told him her cousin Herman had gone to jail when he was eighteen, for murdering his father.

Had she imagined this moment, Adam the one following them deep into the woods instead of her? She's his ghost now, this *Bethie* taunting him about how carefully he lives, how unpredictable the woods can be, how nature can never truly be controlled.

They'd left Toronto for the tenure-track position Elizabeth was offered. *Why do you think I work in cultural sociology and media studies? It's my destiny. I can't escape where I was raised. Better to study it than have it eat you alive. I'm interested in basic human experience, the elemental core of who we are.* She was euphoric about returning to rural Nova Scotia. She said it brought illumination to everyday life. At least they were in the small, cosmopolitan oasis of the university town, a two-hour drive from the redneck county where she grew up, where her family still lived.

The rustle of the leaves beneath their feet form a tiny chorus of mocking voices. Adam had expected it would be slow going, but it's especially slow because the old ladies don't walk very quickly. At least he is able to catch his breath. Charlotte keeps stopping to admire the surroundings and the colour of the leaves. "Oh, the sky reminds me of when I was a young girl. Nothing like a late October sky, is there, Doris?"

Doris isn't interested in the darkening blue sky, now tinged with a bit of gold and mauve. "Charlotte, don't dawdle like some sort of foreigner. We don't have all day."

Charlotte fusses with her angora gloves. "I'm a sentimentalist, I'll have you know. There's not enough sentimentality in this world," she says with an undertone of malice in her voice.

Aunt Doris tries to clear her throat as though something rotten is lodged inside. "There's nothing practical about sentimentality." Adam hears the tremble in Doris's voice. She's always been so steadfast and resilient. Aunt Doris may have been a clerk who specialized in dealing with idiots, but now Adam sees a frail side emerging. Maybe it was always there and he had never noticed. She had expertly concealed it.

"You can't scoop up lost time." Aunt Doris slowly bends over and grabs an armful of paper-thin yellow leaves which immediately spill from her thin arms. She pokes Adam in the ribs with her bony finger and stares at him as though she's never seen him before. But she says what she always says: "It's something, having a Chinaman in the family named Adam O'Malley."

His ancestors came to build the railways across the

country in the 1880s. His grandmother married an Irish immigrant, which is why he has dark eyes and auburn hair, why his mother knew how to play Mahjong, which she learned from her neighbours who had moved to Vancouver before Hong Kong was handed back to the Communists.

"How're your comic books coming along, Adam?"

"Graphic novels, Charlotte."

He should move back to Vancouver, he knows this. But the children are settled. He promised Elizabeth he would let them grow up here.

"That's what they call comic books now? Everything a child needs to know is in Donald Duck," Aunt Doris declares. She sounds more like her old strident self.

Adam thinks how the old ladies wanted you endlessly explaining so the truth would always be in motion.

"Sweet Herman loved reading mysteries. He could have been a writer," Charlotte says, as though Herman is dead and she's remembering him as a young child.

Elizabeth had always said her strange older cousin was an author of sorts, writing on people with his fists instead of a pen. Adam thinks that for all they know, Herman could be dead, but he knows better than to say this out loud and risk Charlotte collapsing in hysterics.

When Elizabeth was bald from the chemo, they took the girls for a visit to Charlotte's place in Nolen,

Elizabeth's childhood village. There were family pictures throughout the house. It was built in the early 1970s but Charlotte always referred to it as *my lovely modern home*. There was a photo on the telephone table of a smiling young teenage Herman holding Elizabeth when she was about five. They had the same dark eyes. Elizabeth adored Herman. His father was Charlotte's eldest child.

Herman had always wanted to inherit the abandoned old family property up on the mountain, Elizabeth had said. The old ladies wouldn't give it to him, not until he turned his life around or theirs ended. If he couldn't get himself on the straight and narrow, as they called it, Herman would just have to wait like a good boy until they died.

The old women continue talking about Herman as they walk, how on the one hand he meant well and on the other hand he was such a misfit. It wasn't his fault he was born this way; his tramp of a mother drank so much when she was pregnant.

Maybe Aunt Doris was right to be suspicious. And maybe Herman's not in jail, he thinks. Adam can't keep track of his incarcerations. "Herman isn't grateful, that's the problem," Aunt Doris says. "If he appreciated even a bit of what people have tried to do for him, if he could just take responsibility, he wouldn't end up in such trouble. Nowadays young people don't want to take responsibility for who they are. Or do penance for their failings."

Another ripple of guilt moves through Adam for doubting Charlotte. He feels like he and Doris are ganging up on a helpless old lady. As the sisters argue, Adam notices how his black leather shoes toss up yellow leaves as he shuffles along.

Charlotte shakes her cane. "No one paid enough attention to poor little Herman," she barks. "And you never had children, so what do you know?"

"Herman's bad in his bones, I've come to believe. Our family has a bad streak," Doris says, with the new warble in her voice. "It's a good thing he's locked up. We're too old to try and help him. And your time has passed for making amends, Charlotte. You should have tried to help him when he was a child. It's too late for regret. You can't fix everything by remembering someone's birthday. You can't unravel the past like you do with your knitting if you miss a stitch."

Charlotte had knit a pink toque for Elizabeth to cover her bald head. Charlotte's own funeral instructions include burying her with her knitting bag. Adam imagines you will hear the *clickity-clackity* of her knitting needles in her pine casket below ground going for as long as her rotting fingers can hold them.

On the way home from that visit, Elizabeth wore the pink toque. The little girls slept in the back of the car.

"How can you stand them?" he asked Elizabeth.

"I think of my life as a Werner Herzog documentary. Herzog says facing the camera is like facing death. That's how I do it. Face life like a camera. Live like I'm in a Herzog film." She was looking straight ahead through the windshield, as if through the night the headlights beamed into a secret she could see but Adam could not, no matter how hard he tried. He remembers gripping the steering wheel in frustration but not saying anything, not wanting to yell at a dying woman or to wake the children.

Werner Herzog is an asshole, he remembers thinking. There was a difference between courage and rashness, between living well and being oblivious to danger. The heater was blasting and he strained to hear Elizabeth as she spoke. Adam remembers how soft her voice was, as though she were praying. Then she was silent for a few minutes before laughing, more like cackling really, and then quiet once more filled the car and all Adam could hear was the low sound of the engine and the heater, the heavy breathing of their small sleeping daughters in their car seats in the back.

When the cancer metastasized to her bones and her brain, Elizabeth wasn't afraid, only angry at the brevity of her lifespan, at the idea of leaving her little girls. She was in a hospice at that stage. Adam remembers there was a photographer who came in to take portraits of the dying. It was for an art show, photographing the dying for the living, a fundraiser for the hospice. Elizabeth loved the concept. The next best thing to Herzog himself, she said. The photographer brought her little boy because she didn't have a babysitter and he played with their girls. But Elizabeth died before the exhibition and Adam didn't go to the opening despite the nice invitations extended. A few months later the photographer had mailed him a sympathy card and a photograph of Elizabeth. She was skeletal and bald but the photographer had captured Elizabeth with a tiny smile as though she had a secret or had finally understood an age-old mystery.

He could still hear Elizabeth's hoarse chemo voice. *I've already faced death. I know what's coming.*

Before she got sick, Elizabeth never expected Adam to come along when she took the old ladies out. She did it only because her mother had made her promise to keep up the family tradition. She was dead too, his mother-in-law, of the same sort of hereditary breast cancer which Elizabeth said she'd been on the watch for.

"We're almost there," Charlotte shouts, waving her cane at a clearing in the trees illuminated by thin, end-of-day sunlight, a dull spotlight on the stage of their memories. There is a massive old apple tree, the wizened apples glowing red, the branches tumbling down like arthritic grey limbs. They walk toward the clearing, the only sound the wind whispering in the leaves.

Elizabeth constantly told him life should be lived in pursuit of what Herzog called *the ecstatic truth*. A truth Adam should hunt for after she was gone if he wanted any real peace of mind. She was very ill by then, but he was still shocked when she died. He hadn't expected the wrath lurching up in his body, an irrational and shameful fury at how Elizabeth had abandoned him with two small, helpless children, as though she had done it on purpose.

Adam knows now it was a terrible fear and sorrow hiding behind the rage. Grief would be tender and quiet, Adam had assumed. But instead he found himself running laps around the pond in the back of the house every night while the children lay asleep in bed, and he hoped they wouldn't wake up alone while he screamed in the woods, fleeing from the stupid ecstatic truth chasing behind him under the dark, sinister sky. Even then the grids and panels in his mind were slipping.

His wife's funeral was packed with friends and colleagues and extended family. Cousin Herman standing at the back of the sanctuary, staring at the coffin. The little girls skipping up and down the aisle between the pews, Aster tripping on the thick red carpet. She hit her chin on the wooden pew and Herman helped her up. She held his big rough hand until she stopped crying.

Then the girls ran up the aisle and sat by the altar, the young priest smiling at them.

Later, at the reception, Aster and Julia asking when Mommy was going to be coming home. Tears leaking from Adam's eyes as Herman put squares and cookies in a plastic bag. *No use good food going to waste*, Herman said. He hadn't shaved or combed his long stringy hair and he was wearing a plaid hunting jacket and work boots. Herman lived in a mobile home near the gravel pit, right by Johnny's Burger.

A few months after the funeral Herman was arrested for punching the mail delivery person.

Adam was stuck with the old women, but at least not with Herman and his stringy hair and his hatred for the mailman who never brought the mail anymore. Herman was like Elizabeth. He did as he pleased, whenever he was so moved, with no hesitation, no regret. Courage or insanity, Adam wasn't sure. They were like backwoods crusaders in an obscure comic. Adam is simultaneously drawn to and repelled by their way of living outside the grid. Nothing ever storyboarded, spontaneity the order of the day, never a glimpse of cowardice or regret.

The old ladies blamed Elizabeth's cancer on her life-style—the tree planting she did in the clear-cuts high up in northern British Columbia, exposure to some sort of pesticide. If she had stayed in Nova Scotia with a normal job none of it would have happened. They viewed her education as something that had made her vulnerable, a thing which stole her inborn wisdom and replaced it with disease. Elizabeth said it was genetics, an inherited genome triggered by who knows what, a demon lying in wait. At first she was sure she wouldn't die, but then she knew she would stop breathing in the hospital bed, her lungs full of fluid, the "Get well soon, Mommy" drawings on the wall like posters in a kindergarten class.

Adam doesn't want to think about Elizabeth's death throes anymore. He takes a deep breath. "Ladies, we should turn back," Adam says firmly, rubbing his hands together because he is very cold now. He hears a sound but he isn't sure what it is, almost like water. Maybe they are closer to the bay than he thought, and it's been lurking there the entire time and only now the tide is high and the white caps are crashing on the shore. "We really need to turn back before night falls. I need to pick the girls up at the babysitter's house."

But Charlotte and Doris carry on as though they don't hear him. None of this was part of the day's plan. Adam now worries they'll be stumbling back in the dark. If the battery dies on his cellphone they won't even have a flashlight. A hatred for technology fills him, how he's become so dependent on one small rectangle. Adam fears they'll go off the path into the woods and then fall into a ravine. Or tumble off a cliff and crash into the bay below. "Look, I really don't mean to rush you but it's a work day for me tomorrow. I have to go home. My daughters are waiting for me. I had no idea how long this would take."

It is almost as though he could hear Elizabeth scoff about his need for a plan. *Werner Herzog says storyboards are for cowards.* It was why she lived her life from moment to moment, why even with the children she hated a routine. Why she had not gone to the doctor when she first found the lump. His terror at losing his beloved wife has been replaced by a bottomless hole of thick loss.

The sun is lowering quickly. Adam looks at his phone. Still no signal.

And then he sees it—further into the clearing, the remains of the stone foundation of the old house. It's now full of brown grasses and dwarfed by overgrown lilac bushes along its edges, their decaying blossoms like black spears at the top of the high branches.

"We need to go back." Adam keeps repeating this, his voice vibrating, the words falling off his dry tongue.

"A cup of tea would be nice. Your wife always brought a thermos of tea. And fresh biscuits. She was such a sweet, thoughtful young thing, even with that one hard year she had." Charlotte gives him her sly grin again. "Did Bethie ever tell you about how when she was a teenager she got sent to the youth detention centre? She punched a girl right in the head. Gave her a concussion. Bethie beat her to a pulp. And you go on about Herman having bad blood, Doris."

"Charlotte, my land! That's ancient history. Adam doesn't need to know. Bethie was a good girl. She was a sweet thing. She had spirit. Bethie was a one-of-a-kind girl."

The shadows falling on the ground seem alive, everything spilling outside his field of vision in a full bleed. Adam can't force this new information or this moment into a grid even though he keeps trying and trying. Elizabeth had said only that she was a tomboy growing up, how she couldn't stand being teased. There is no gutter between the panels, no empty space between images. The panels won't even take shape. Adam has no control over time here. He's trapped in a documentary film about his life and it can't even be neatly edited. His heart thuds, his breath frantic like Elizabeth's when she was in labour with the girls, panting like an animal. An owl hoots. Far off, a coyote yips. The old ladies have been talking the whole time Adam has been thinking. Their chatter is as constant as the dry leaves whispering in the forest.

Adam looks up, beyond the overgrown foundation, and spots a small weathered wooden shack to the north of the clearing, behind a thin stand of firs. "I'm going to say again we need to turn back, ladies. We're going to be stranded out here in the dark." His breath steams out in the chilly air.

Charlotte looks toward the fir trees and back to the path. "But it's Herman's birthday. He likes to come into the woods. It's where he goes during the hunting season."

"But he's in jail . . . isn't he?" Aunt Doris asks again. She's now completely uncertain. Maybe she was always uncertain, and Adam can finally see it—this part of him which agreed to the insanity of this trip also hears thoughts, tastes fear, senses heartbeats and can see through masks. He was blind before, that was the prob-lem. He just saw what he wanted, but not the whole picture. There was a safe border around everything, but now there is a bleed to the edge. Adam can't stand this. He tries to think in panels, but none come to him. He sniffs the air like a beast sensing danger.

"I have to pick up my children from the babysitter. Tomorrow's a work day. How many times do I have to say this? For the last time, let's turn around." The anger in his voice echoes through the clearing.

The bushes shake and there is the sound of branches and twigs snapping. A cold breeze blows on their faces. Herman walks out from behind the high dead bushes. The surprise in those familiar dark eyes narrows into fury.

"Lookee what we have here." Herman's strange,

angry laughter booms out into the clearing in sharp bursts.

"He's out of jail? Charlotte, you horrible person, you knew."

"I just want to have a visit with my oldest grandchild, Doris. Oh, Herman, I'm sorry it's been so hard for you. But we came all this way for your birthday. And I brought Aunt Doris, just like you said to." Charlotte begins to warble "Happy Birthday" in a grotesque voice.

Charlotte is delusional. Adam wonders how he could possibly have missed her senility, how Doris too must have looked the other way, made excuses and justified her sister's irrationality, her odd changes.

Doris tries to smile but she can't quiet manage it and gives Herman a grimace. "Your grandmother is confused, Herman dear. We don't want any trouble."

"Shut up, you filthy old bag. I *am* trouble. You come looking for me, you get what you come looking for."

Charlotte's face crumples. She brushes a blood-red leaf off her dress. "Herman, you're a good boy. You just always like to march to the beat of your own drum."

"Ain't it the truth. You just march right back here with me, Grandma. Back around behind the bushes. You too, Aunt Doris, you dirty, rickety spinster." Herman grabs them each by an arm. Charlotte falls and he pulls her to her feet. She sobs but she lets Herman lead her forward. Doris struggles and he twists her arm. She whimpers. All at once, Adam can move, and he takes a step.

Herman waves his fist at Adam and growls. "Now you, boy, get going. Or else."

"Or else what? Let them go, Herman."

The old ladies are both crying.

Herman lets go of their arms, bends down and picks up a shotgun from behind the high bushes. He points it at Adam.

"You know you don't belong here, boy. You go home to the little girls. I'll count to three and if you're still here then you won't leave me with no choice but to start with you. So let's see you run like a dog. I'll give you a head start while I take care of the ladies. Then I'll come after you."

Adam runs. He has a plan. He will run like a dog and call 911.

Night looms down. Adam lurches back along the path that had once been a road, the dry roar of leaves at his feet muffling the gunshots.

The wind slithers in the branches and moans through the woods. Adam sees the ecstatic truth has been inside him the whole time. He howls at the trees. He doesn't know how many gunshots fire behind him, if there were one or two or three shots, or if there have been any gunshots at all, if Herman is thrashing through the woods after him, because Adam is breathing so hard he can only hear his heart hammering in his ears, the blood bashing in his brain, and his own voice screaming and echoing back *I am Werner Herzog, I am Werner Herzog* as he comes out on the road under the early stars in the indigo sky. Still no signal but Adam screams "I am Werner Herzog" into his phone when he dials 911 even though it doesn't connect, still screaming this once his phone finally picks up a signal as he drives along the dirt road and along the top of the dark mountain which drops down and bleeds into the valley of cowards below.

OCCLUSION

THE WORLD LOOKS DIFFERENT upside down. The blood pounding behind my eyes and my unusual position distort perspective. There is no natural light. I can't tell if what I'm seeing is real. I picture myself in a photo, me strapped into some sort of industrial swivel chair, half naked, with my right breast hanging out.

I've never been upside down this long, not as a child on playground equipment and not as an adult in a yoga class. Not in the park with Saul, my six-year-old, wanting me to hang from my creaky knees while singing "Ode to Billie Joe," a song Saul's grandmother taught him when she still took care of him, before my father's dementia took over.

I was given a sedative before the procedure because I was having an anxiety attack. I'm already on anti-anxiety medication and antidepressants, prescribed right after Saul's father died. And I'm on medication for neuropathic pain from a car accident I had when Saul was three and I was hurrying to a meeting after dropping him at daycare. My body seems to have recovered from the whiplash and concussion, but my neurology hasn't. Now add this nice pill from the nurses and my mind is wandering and dreamy, my thoughts drifting clouds.

My poor mother. I remember when she started putting little Saul in front of the television, turning up the volume to drown out my father's almost constant yelling, directed everywhere and at everyone except my son. We don't fully understand why, but he doesn't perceive a small child as a threat. His outbursts increased as his world began to dim. A thin shadow falling on the hardwood floor by the hearth was a treacherous ghost. He would put his false teeth in the bread box and would cry when he noticed his teeth were gone, accusing my mother of pulling them out while he slept. A small noise seemed an explosion to him, and suddenly he was lost in the Korean War. He would scoop Saul up, lurching out the door and into the woods as he moved into a realm we could not perceive.

Saul wasn't afraid. He has always seen his grandfather as a man living between two worlds. As my father's worlds became narrow and distorted, so too did our perspective change—the day-to-day magnified, separated out from the bigger picture, as though we were living with tunnel vision, trying to survive one more sundown.

And now I'm stuck in this chair, upended, stoned, unable to see anything clearly.

THE NURSE, CLARA, HAS said we'll be underway any moment but that was a while ago...I think. I would know Clara's voice anywhere. She has a way of laughing at the end of her sentences, even when she's upset. I took her daughter's photos when she was born. Right now I can't even imagine holding a camera—I can see only inside myself, strapped here, waiting, my memories emerging as though my unusual position has jostled them from where they were sealed.

I took the portraits of Clara's newborn last year up on the maternity floor. Instead of taking the elevator I walked up the three flights of stairs. There was no time for exercising. Helping my family as well as single-parenting was overwhelming. It was a triumph to make it through each day. Walking up the stairs seemed like a way to multi-task and cross exercise off my endless "to do" list. My heart pounded and my footsteps echoed in the stairwell. I was gasping for breath and had to stand at the top of the stairs, composing myself. Most people forget that hospital staff have personal lives, their own joys and sorrows. It is one of my jobs for money to support my art photography, helping parents create memory books of the birth day. Doing a photo story for them. Helping them write poems and short personal essays to accompany the photos.

This morning I was in the outer waiting room when Clara came to get me and bring me to the inner waiting room, where I was deposited into a little stall and given a johnny gown and a robe. It seems like days ago I was in the little stall but it has only been a few hours. I must have taken a long time because a woman who wasn't Clara asked if I was okay. I came out and she pointed to a chair. I recognized Matilda then. She's near retirement. Her children are grown, but one of her daughters fell off a cliff over at the shore when she was four. How do you ever get over that? Sometimes Matilda gives community talks about child safety. My friend Athena interviewed her once for a national radio program on grief.

Athena was supposed to drive me to the hospital for this procedure, but I've been so anxious I gave her the wrong date. I texted her from the taxi on my way here and she said she'd get off work and drive out to the hospital as soon as she could. Athena always keeps her word. When you have a best friend like her there isn't much more in life you need—except good health.

Athena is six feet tall and has waist-length black hair. She's a radio producer and lives in the city. She travels a lot with her work. Her great-grandfather came from Lebanon. When she introduces herself as Athena people correct her and say she must be from Greece. Athena laughs at this. She thinks it's funny how I call myself the "panini generation" because it's cooler than "sandwich." Athena would see the humour in how long I've been dangling upside down, waiting and waiting for the tests to start.

IT WAS GOOD TO hear Clara's familiar voice. I hadn't known she worked in the day surgery unit. The hospital clothes are pale and smell chemical-fresh. The same smell from when I gave birth to Saul, six years ago — institutional and oddly comforting.

I sniffed the folded johnny gown before taking off my sweater and bra, then stripped naked except for panties. I cradled the pile of green, could almost feel Saul as a newborn in my arms, see him jaundiced and yellow, wrapped in a white cloth which smelled just like the gown. We were in hospital for a week after he was born.

But that was another time here, in a different ward.

ATHENA AND I BECAME friends when she attended my photography show *Portraits of Grief* at a gallery in

Halifax. Her niece was in one of the photos. Saul was just a baby then and I had brought him along. He slept in his baby carrier.

I texted Athena when I got the results back from the first mammogram. *Abnormal.* Athena had been in Toronto at a meeting. She had stepped into the hall and called me on my cell. "Don't worry. It's probably nothing, Honeycakes."

This is Athena's nickname for both me and Saul.

Then the second test was abnormal, too.

They sent a letter both times. For efficiency. Clarity. So it's in black and white.

It was a cold day, with a little late-March snow on the ground. The sky was low and grey. The grass was brown and the tree branches were bleak. It was splendid nonetheless. I texted Athena, who called again. I was crying this time. "Could I have chemo and keep working?"

Athena was quiet. "Sure." Then she cleared her throat. "Are you fucking crazy, Daisy? Do you know how hard that will be?"

I was quiet. Just my gulping breath.

"If you push yourself, maybe," Athena said.

More silence. We both know I'm self-employed. No insurance.

"It's probably nothing," she said. "But if it's something, it's probably treatable."

RIGHT NOW I'M UPSIDE down and Clara is talking but I can't make out the words. It's hard to hear upside down. I feel safer with my eyes closed so I can retreat to my inner terrain. Deep breathing... four counts for each breath, a hold before exhaling, a hold before inhaling. If you can control your breath and heart, you've got it made. This is what I've been learning in the community mindful yoga and meditation classes my doctor recommended. Still, my heart pounds and the blood whooshes by my ear canals. When they tip me back around, the blood will pour out of my mouth, a libation to the gods.

A prayer for good genes. For my breasts to be healthy.

MAYBE THEY REALLY HAVE forgotten me. The chirping machines, dinging gadgets, and computerized charts hold their attention, not me, Upside Down Daisy.

While immobilized like this, the last person I want to think about is my sister, Ruth, but of course she forces her way into my mind just as she forces her way into my life. My sister Ruth always says people can't escape the clutches of their past. She says, in her superior way, that if you apply her formula, you can hold off grief or catastrophe, melancholy, dementia, or blindness. She's a physiotherapist and she tells all her patients they'll recover if they do the exercises *exactly* how and when she tells them.

Ruth's thirty-five, eleven years younger than I am. There was a brother in between but he died shortly after he was born. He had a hole in his heart. Ruth says she's lived her life in his shadow. My father couldn't get over his disappointment that she was a girl. Ruth says she should have been born first because I'm so immature and make such bad choices she has to act like a big sister. Ruth has never stopped telling our mother this. It makes her cry but Ruth doesn't care. In fact, it's her goal.

It's like Ruth is a horrible self-help book I've absorbed, and while I'm waiting captive here in this hospital room, mean things Ruth has said or done appear in my mind the way spring ducks come flying in and land on a pond. I'm so cold and my body hurts so much being suspended like this, and I can't get Ruth out of my mind.

There is a metallic taste in my mouth. Blood—I've bitten my lip, still tense even with the drugs. Maybe the sedative is wearing off. A few tears well up and I blink them away. The artist in me takes over and I see the entire horizon of my life shaded with the tone of her words.

IT'S MOSTLY OUR FATHER'S fault, according to Ruth. It's the patriarchy. Two girls. He wanted boys. I have a child, *out of wedlock*, as Ruth calls it—but our father is thrilled Saul has our last name. Ruth married a successful lawyer and Dad's happy she took his last name. She always says our father views my patched-together work as *entrepreneurial*. She has to be the girl in the family for both of us, be overlooked for two, invisibility times two.

It's hard to argue with her. After our father was diagnosed with Alzheimer's disease he took his big orange cat and seat-belted it in the passenger seat beside him. He went off for a drive and came back a bit later, saying Ruthie was hungry.

"Dad," I said. "That's the cat, not Ruth."

My son giggled behind his hands, his dark brown eyes peering over his little fingertips.

"What in god's name is the cat doing in the car?" My father unbuckled the cat.

Remarkably, the cat seemed to enjoy the outing.

It enraged Ruth. "You're all ending up with problems, and I have to take care of you."

Ruth's husband is the only one who has patience with her. She had a late-term miscarriage. A stillbirth is what it was. Her husband called me that night and I drove to the city. Ruth couldn't even look at me, she was crying so hard. "Why do you get to have a child?" That's all she said.

"Ruth doesn't mean it, Daisy," her husband said as he wept. But we both know she did.

A faraway voice says my name. It's not Ruth or her husband, but Nurse Clara telling me to hang on; she knows how disorienting it is, how upsetting. There seems to be some trouble with the equipment. She rubs my shoulder but I keep my eyes closed. I remember again that I'm drugged, which is why it's so hard to be present.

"TIME IS PASSING," RUTH informed me on the phone when I told her about my first test results, the ones which led to the second mammogram. And then the second mammogram, which led to this third, more invasive, drawn-out testing to see if I have cancer.

When I told my sister about the first test results I hoped it would open her eyes a little, that she would understand that I, too, have problems and that it isn't as easy as she thinks for me to help our parents as much as I do. "It's probably your own fault," Ruth said instead. "From drinking too much coffee or something. You must have done something to cause this." I could hear that Ruth was trying not to cry, anger being easier than fear and cruelty easier than vulnerability. But that didn't mean she was going to change her view of me.

Ever since our father took a pot of coffee and poured

it on a plate and was subsequently diagnosed, every-thing has been my fault. Now that our mother is having problems with her right eye, Ruth has turned her panic against me.

"You live closer. You're right there, so why can't you be their caregiver?" Ruth demands. Ruth would have made better choices if she'd been born first, she always tells me. I should have been the youngest, the reckless and irresponsible one. I've even robbed Ruth of her place in the family.

She thinks Saul should have been given up for adoption. His father is a loser, she'll say when she's upset. *Your boyfriend.* She never even called him my partner when he was alive. Ruth said once that it was repre-hensible for us to reproduce. We had bad genes. Our genetic legacy was one of curses.

Even though our mother rarely calls Ruth for help, Ruth is totally convinced she's doing everything on her own. "Why can't they call you," she says, "when there's trouble?"

"They do. I drive over there and Saul sits in the car in his pyjamas."

"How hard can it be to be a single parent?"

No matter how often it's explained to her that I do as much as she does, Ruth denies it. Her husband views this as how Ruth copes with loss, through a prism of rage.

Thinking about Ruth makes me feel sick. But it could be the drugs.

IT WAS A WEEK before this third testing when my mother called me about her eyesight problem. I drove to my parents' house to find that Ruth was already there. She had arrived for an unannounced visit. She'd taken a day off and come out to the country to buy some wool for her new rug-hooking hobby.

They didn't hear me come in. I stood in the porch. Ruth was on a roll to my mother, who couldn't get a word in: "Crazy Daisy is too indulgent, Mum, you know this. I work full-time in a *real job* as a physiotherapist, and I have a *husband*. He's a *lawyer*. People *depend* on us. People with *actual* problems. Middle-aged people should be *independent*. What is *wrong* with Daisy? How can we even be related?

"Who has a baby at *forty*? And who *mates* with a loser who *dies drunk and stoned* in a car when his child is only three and leaves behind a mountain of online gambling debt?" In that moment in the porch, it was as though I was hearing Ruth describe someone I didn't know, an obtuse woman who was blind to the reality of her life.

I wish I could leap out of this chair and run away and leave myself behind. But my arms and legs are numb. I can hardly move them.

A DOOR OPENS. FOOTSTEPS. I wish for it to be Athena but it isn't.

"Do you mind if he sits in?" Clara says.

It's so cold. I open my eyes and all I can see is a bright light. I hardly slept last night. Maybe exhaustion is making time slow down. Making the past flash before my eyes.

"Do I mind if who sits in?"

My voice breaks. It's not tears. It's the blood in my head. I wiggle but my right breast is clamped into the machine. It is a preposterous position. My johnny gown keeps falling away and Clara tucks my ass back in. They're trying to find the right position to crush my tit, to scan it, so they can find the spot the second mammogram had caught. The abnormality.

But locating the exact spot is proving unusually difficult.

"The medical student. Do you mind if he joins us?" Clara is kind, extra kind. She remembers when I took her family portrait. Clara thinks I'm about to cry. I might cry. I'd wanted it so badly to be Athena who walked into the room, her low voice reassuring me it would all be okay. Maybe crying would help me relax. I haven't decided yet. It's hard to decide anything in this position.

They know they should have checked with me earlier, not assumed. A man kneels down now. In blue scrubs and wearing thick glasses and a face mask. "I'm a medical student. Ian. Is it okay?" He sounds young.

"The more the merrier." Spots in my eyes now. I might pass out.

Ian-the-medical-student laughs. "I see you have a sense of humour."

My friend Athena would approve of Ian. Humour is our shield, Athena always says.

"What's that about a shield?" Ian asks.

At first I don't know what he's talking about and then realize I'm so disoriented in this position I'm thinking out loud, quietly speaking Athena's words of wisdom.

The specialist speaks. When did he come in? "Sorry we have you in this position. It's a bit hard to get your breast in the right spot, with the suspicious area in the inside corner like it is. And your breast is small. You're so thin."

MY MISTAKES HANG AROUND my neck, a garland of shame I'm sure everyone in town can see when I walk holding Saul's hand as we take the path which cuts through the back streets to the library. *There goes Crazy Daisy*, they probably say. Saul wants to take laneways and alleys. He likes to lead the way. When we moved out of the city, I rented a small house on a dead-end street full of retired people who might not approve but who have enough life behind them to knit some pity in with their judgment. The house was built in the seventies, the landlord told me when he showed it to me. He was a commercial property developer and this was his only residential rental. For a particular kind of tenant, a word-of-mouth tenant, he said. It was his parents' retirement home. He couldn't bear to sell it now that they had passed away. He lived in a huge house across the street.

He almost wept when he said they had passed away.

The back room facing the huge lawn and garden had been his father's study. There was a woodstove. He would leave it in for me.

Athena had recommended me. Her uncle is friends with my landlord and her recommendation was all it took. It was hard to explain my unusual work of free-lance photography, art shows, and workshops. You do what you can to make a living when you have a fine arts degree.

The landlord already knew I worked for the hospital part-time. I didn't tell him it wasn't actually a job; it was just a grant the hospital kept getting renewed every year, for me to take portraits of mothers and their babies. He said it was noble work.

The 1970s house has not been renovated since it was built, except that my landlord replaced the windows and ripped out the orange shag carpet. But it has the original appliances and the original tile and fixtures in the bathroom. It may be a bit shabby now, dated, but no expense was spared when it was custom built, made for easy living. You lose sense of time when you walk into the porch. The world falls away. Life is gentler. The past is framed with blurry nostalgia.

Nostalgia feels like a distant luxury to me, though, suspended here in the terror of the present and what this test might reveal. It's been so hard living as a single parent, having this little child who depends on me and me alone ever since his father died. Little Saul's artist mother, living hand to mouth, trying to pay the bills and keep at her art, looking after her parents, keeping Ruthie at arm's length. I suddenly realize how terrified I am of dying, how I feel I can't even die, there are so many people depending on me.

THE FIRST MAMMOGRAM HAD been in a cold room just down the hall. I stood there while my breast was crushed flat. Any sense of being a sexy woman was squashed along with it. They don't tell you ahead of time what breastfeeding does to your breasts, how they dangle and seem deflated, empty sacks, the result of two years of nursing. They said breast-feeding helped reduce the risk of cancer. I thought it was insurance.

The technician and the nurse said it could very well be calcium deposits. Or scar tissue. Maybe I had banged my breast at some point in my life. The dots in the mammogram reading were like salt and pepper flecks. These weren't as concerning, they weren't as dense. That was reassuring. We'd do another scan and hopefully it would show nothing.

After the second abnormal results, my family doctor called me to set up the core biopsy. "It could be nothing," she said, her face noncommittal. "The core biopsy will tell us. Remember, breast cancer is a treatable disease most of the time."

She squeezed my shoulder. "Try to relax. Keeping doing yoga."

But I'm sure being upside down like this is not what she meant.

THE DOCTORS HERE ARE all men and even though I can't see their faces, their voices are kind when they speak to me, as though they know how disturbing it is that I can't see their eyes. My sister has little time for most men.

"Look at that Brazilian soccer player," she says. "He killed his wife and fed her to his Rottweilers and people still love him. He's out of jail now, a team signed him, and he wants his child back."

Somehow Ruth has still managed to find the perfect man. My brother-in-law is huge and muscular and tattooed. His voice booms when he speaks. He has a buzz cut. He was raised by his grandparents and he cries easily. He volunteers with a feral cat rescue program. He knows how to knit. He worked on lobster boats until he was in his late twenties. When he saw the men around him crippled up with arthritis by the time they were in their early fifties, he said he didn't want to grow old before his time. He fished on weekends and went to university during the week. He read his textbooks on the boat. His uncles and cousins teased him but not very much. They were proud. He never gave up. That's their family motto, I always think: *Never Give Up*.

"What a good attitude, Daisy." One of the doctors is speaking.

I must have spoken out loud again, my brother-in-law's adage coming out of my mouth.

SUSPICIOUS.

That's the word they use.

It could mean nothing.

"With two mammograms indicating an abnormality, we need to find out." It's yet another nurse assisting the doctor. Not Clara. I can't keep track of who is in the room anymore. At this stage it's not a technician, although a technician is present. It's the radiologist. He's already explained that for a core biopsy they use the mammogram and an X-ray machine, to make sure they get the correct tissue to send to the pathologist.

"We locate the area, based on both previous sets of scans. The ones which showed the spot."

"How are things?" the nurse asks. "We're just going to make this a little tighter. Sorry for the discomfort. Do you feel okay?"

Then they take out my breast and sit me up. The blood rushes down. I pray for good results.

And then they move the chair again, and the machine, and clamp me back in.

I say it feels as though I'm seeing a dentist, chiropractor, and massage therapist all at the same time. They laugh.

Clara asks me if I have plans for Easter. It's March already but there is still snow on the ground. It's been a long winter. I'm taking a few days off. Taking my son to the city, to the pool.

ATHENA SENT ME A card in the middle of all the waiting for tests. She's that kind of person, who still sends cards and surprise packages in the mail. *You just have to learn to be in the space in-between and keep going,* she wrote. *You have to be in your life for your child. You can't postpone life*. Athena gets frustrated by wasted life, as she calls it. She had a double mastectomy five years ago. Her scans have all been clear. People forget, Athena says. They have scares and then cradle the moment like a newborn baby, smell the unmistakable freshness. And then they just forget.

THE SUMMER SAUL WAS four, the summer just before his father died, he would wait in the window for his father to pick him up. He was usually late and sometimes forgot. But that one summer he remembered and was always on time. He'd pick Saul up at four o'clock and bring him back at seven, dropping him in the driveway and leaving without talking to me. I never really knew what Saul did with his father on those summer evenings. Saul would make up stories about incredible fishing trips and backwoods expeditions. I wasn't surprised he was making them up. That is what children do when they need love, when they wish for reality to be something other than it is. I was mostly surprised I almost believed his stories. It was his longing I believed, because longing never lies. Saul would weep. I would put him in a warm bath. "There, there," I said. "It will get better."

The big lie.

His father died six months later.

It was the summer grief pressed in upon me in the way a watermark imprints paper, permanent and imperceptible in certain light.

THE DOCTOR IS TALKING.

"It's a core biopsy because we go into the core of the area of concern. We put a needle in, and then insert an even smaller needle through the tube, if you can visualize this. And then we remove a tiny strand of tissue. We repeat this quite a few times, to get enough tiny strands. Then we X-ray the strands. And we send the tissue to the pathologist."

It's probably three hours they've had me strapped in here, flipping me around for a few breaks in position. Poking at my breast. Jabbing over and over again, the extraction of the vermicelli tissues. They keep complimenting me on my composure.

Clara squeezes my hand a few times. "How's your neck? We tried to be careful because of your whiplash. Have a big soak in the tub with Epsom salts tonight. Do you have a ride home? You can't drive," she says.

"Athena is coming." I close my eyes as they poke some more.

Then I think of the newborn photos I have taken in the child and maternity ward.

"THAT'S IT," CLARA SAYS, and then taps me on the shoulder. "Did you fall asleep? That would be a first." She smiles as she looks away. I remember how she held her dead baby, so perfect and still. She wasn't crying when we took the photos. Clara wanted the pictures. The only ones she'd have to remember her daughter by, so it wouldn't just be in her mind's eye.

BACK IN THE CHANGING area Clara bandages my breast. It's different from when I gave birth. Saul was born a month early. It didn't matter who saw me with my legs spread wide open, blood and amniotic fluid dripping out. Or breastfeeding, my porn star boobs, as I called them, huge and swollen, trying to get the baby to latch. It would help with his jaundice. Saul's father came in only once that week. It was just as well. I was exhausted. The baby nursed every two hours, day and night. He went under the ultraviolet lights to help eliminate the bilirubin causing his jaundice. My breasts would leak as I reached my hand through the small opening in the incubator to stroke his little belly.

I was in a semi-private room and my roommate had lost her baby. The hospital was so overcrowded they couldn't give her a private room. One of the maternity nurses had seen *Life*, a photography show I'd had at the Hardware Gallery, a small art gallery near the hospital here in Kentville. *Life* was a series of portraits of people in the local hospice. The maternity nurse delicately asked me about taking portraits once she found out I was the photographer who had done the show about the dying. I agreed to take the photos of the stillborn baby. It put into perspective Saul's jaundice, even my strained relationship with his father. It can always be worse. That's what Athena says.

ATHENA ARRIVES AS CLARA leaves to answer a page over the intercom. "Honeycakes," she says, patting my hair, looking at the blood-soaked johnny gown and robe on the floor which Clara hasn't picked up yet. Matilda, the older nurse, comes in and puts the dirty clothes in a basket. She leaves as the doctor arrives. He gawks at Athena like she's famous. She has that effect on people.

The doctor composes himself. They couldn't see the right tissue when they X-rayed the strands of flesh they extracted, he says. It was such an awkward location to do a core biopsy on. The pathologist will probably tell them to call me back in to do the test again. Or they might just do a surgical biopsy and remove the whole area.

"That's a lumpectomy, though, isn't that what you're saying?" Athena isn't pleased. She thinks they've been sloppy. She feels the testing is getting too invasive too quickly when they don't even know what they're dealing with yet.

The doctor nods. "Well, yes, that's true, but we'd be doing it as a biopsy."

Clara comes back in and puts the bandages in the garbage. "It is impossible to know how these tests will go ahead of time."

"It was unusual for it to be this hard to get a tissue sample," the doctor says with a sympathetic look on his face.

Clara rubs her hand on my arm.

The doctor leaves.

Athena says she'll wait outside.

Clara says through the closed drapes as I dress how she wanted to tell me how much she still loves the photos. When I started taking the post-mortem portraits here, she says, she never imagined I would be taking pictures of her baby. Clara says she has the prints in a small white satin album. She looks at them only occasionally now, a year later. The first few months she looked at them on the hour.

ATHENA DRIVES ME HOME. We talk about facials and yoga, about novels and podcasts. The pale blue sky is an immense eye before us.

I tell Athena about the photos I took of Clara's little

daughter. How she had died in utero the day before she was born. Clara was induced and gave birth to her dead little girl. They called me in. I came and took portraits of the baby, bundled up. And the baby in her parents' arms. It isn't technical skill you need as much as compassion and empathy, an ability to see beauty in unexpected places. To see the baby as a baby, not as a corpse.

Athena cries a little as she drives.

It's hard to explain to someone who has never lost a child this way. The parents are still parents. It's still their baby. Their beloved. They existed. Post-mortem photography was commonplace in the Victorian era, even in the early twentieth century. And now pathologists photograph corpses as a routine part of autopsy. And people like me come with a camera and a quiet voice, and capture those first and final moments of love.

My brother-in-law had me photograph their little dead baby. His name was Simon and he was so tiny, born far too soon. Ruthie still can't talk about him. She looks at the photos, though, my brother-in-law says. Those photos remind her that, even if briefly, she too was a mother.

THE DAY AFTER THE upside-down ordeal, my entire breast is swollen and bruised. It's shocking when I take the bandage off. All night, whenever I roll on it, the throbbing pain wakes me up. The pricks aren't even visible, they were so tiny, but my breast screams at each assault. When Saul comes barging in I have to cover it up so he won't be frightened.

Saul goes to school and I go to visit my parents. They don't know about the mammograms, the core biopsy.

My mother is in the kitchen having a drink. She points at her eye. It's an ocular occlusion, she says. This is why she's been seeing things in shades of indigo. The doctor said the vein will occlude. It will collapse. It is going to close off the blood flow. She will lose the sight in the eye and there is nothing they can do. The doctor said she'll adjust to having vision in only one eye.

Dad is outside burning garbage in the burn barrel. I never argue with him about creating pollution and the diminishing ozone layer. He is a man of his time and will never see things any other way than the way he sees them.

He pokes the fire with a long stick and black smoke curls up into the air. "Your mother drinks too much," my father says. "That's what's wrong with her blood pressure. And her eye. You look, under the sink. All those Mason jars of vinegar she's got there? That's not vinegar for cleaning. I don't put them there. Your mother does. They won't believe me now, will they, not with half my brain closing down." He sounds more lucid than he has in weeks.

I leave him stirring his burn barrel and go inside and sniff the vodka in the jars under the sink. My mother comes in from the living room. "I can't stop him from drinking. It's not my fault. It's the only thing he's got left. Can't you see what's going on, Daisy?" The truth is obscured for me. Maybe they're both drinking out of Mason jars.

A WEEK LATER, THE hospital calls before Saul and I are up for breakfast. They leave a voice mail message to say a woman is in the hospital labouring, and can I come in and take photos. They expect the stillbirth by breakfast time, from the way she's progressing. The baby died two days earlier; this is the soonest they were able to schedule the inducement.

A spring hoarfrost has coated the lawn, trees, and fence in magnificent ferny white ice crystals. The driveway is slippery. I carefully get Saul off to school and head to the hospital. My cellphone rings in my purse as I'm parking the car. I shut the engine off and answer. It's my family doctor with the results of my core biopsy.

She gives me my test results while I sit in the hospital parking lot.

"They did get enough of those tiny strands of flesh. It was nothing. It was just calcium deposits," my doctor says. "Enjoy the rest of your day, Daisy."

I call Athena. It goes to voice mail, so I leave a message. The phone rings. Ruthie.

"Everything is fine," I tell her.

I hear Ruth take a deep breath and exhale slowly.

Then she talks: "Wow. Maybe we aren't cursed."

Next Ruth cries: "I'm so sorry, Daisy. It's hard seeing things how you do. Maybe we can have Saul on a weekend in the city so you can have a break. If you'll trust him with us. I know you're a good mother. When Mum and Dad die, you'll be the only one left in the family for me to look up to. I hope you see that."

What I see is how frightened I've always been to be the oldest, to be responsible for others. Worrying how Ruth will never unwind or soften. But we must keep going, even when we're afraid. This is what it is to be brave, and if you're lucky, you'll have one good friend at your side.

I head into the hospital, to the child and maternity unit. When I walk into the new mother's room with my camera bag, she's holding the baby, who is swaddled in a delicate crocheted blanket.

I sit in the small chair at the side of the room and

take out my camera. It is sometimes luck. Sometimes genetics. Many times there are no reasons that will ever make sense.

The woman holds out her baby with the tiny brown face against the soft blue wool. "I don't know why she died," she says. She's weeping. "Isn't she beautiful?"

Her husband sobs beside her. He wipes his eyes, and his wife's. He holds his wife as she cradles the infant. Then everything is completely silent for a moment as they gaze at their baby.

"My beauty."

I hold the camera up to one eye, closing the other, like my mother, adjusting to a new perspective.

LATE AND SOON

EDMUND JUMPING OFF THE garage roof...do you remember? Soaring to the earth and landing with a smile. We wanted to be him, even just for a moment. Edmund and his friend Ian headed off to the barn, leaving the ladder against the garage wall. We climbed and clung to the edge of the garage roof. We were five years old. Edmund, he was nine. We peered down from the roof over the field across the treetops to Cape Blomidon and the Minas Basin at low tide, blue sky plunging into the red mud. The leaves were falling so quickly then.

We were scared without Edmund. You reached for the ladder and knocked it over. How would we get down? "Wait a minute," you whispered. "No," I said and jumped. I heard my arm break. Do you remember how hard you cried? Your face was purple, the colour you told me your penis turned sometimes. You'd told me in church, how your penis turned purple like the velvet robe the minister wore. I didn't have a penis, you told me. This was the main reason we weren't identical. I was born so quickly and then you took two more hours to come into the world. Dad nicknamed us "Late" and "Soon."

You were screaming as you looked down at me from the garage roof. Edmund heard us all the way from the barn and came back to find me lying there on the grass by the fallen ladder. He carried me home with you weeping at his side. Dad and Edmund took me to the emergency room. Dad recited Wordsworth poems while he drove, to distract me. Remember how much he loved the English Romantics? He would have been a scholar in a different life, Mum always said. As Dad carried me into the hospital, he kept repeating, "A host of golden daffodils beside the lake, beneath the trees, fluttering and dancing in the breeze. Don't cry, little Soon," he said. "You're strong."

REMEMBER WHEN WE WERE fifteen, picking apples after school? Edmund picked us up when we were finished in the orchard. It was already getting dark when we came home that Tuesday and Mum wasn't making supper as she always did at that time of day. She was reading a magazine, having a cup of tea with her apron on. She told us Dad had dressed in his suit and tie for work that morning like he always did and left for the canning plant. But then he'd called in the afternoon. He had checked into the Cornwallis Inn in Kentville because he needed time alone, time to sort things out. He was depressed and needed a break, she told us as she flipped through the magazine without looking up. He wanted us to come down for supper, just us, he didn't need her to come — she could stay home alone, have some time to herself. I think she was relieved. All summer he'd been quiet. She sipped her tea and ate a cookie. It was a Pim's, a biscuit from France with orange jam filling. Mum loved them. Edmund was nineteen. He drove us to the hotel in his red pickup truck. He'd come home from firefighter practice just to take us.

DO YOU REMEMBER THE old daphne shrub out by the barn which flowered each spring? Dad moved to the hotel a few weeks after Mum found the Cajun woman from New Orleans sitting beside the blooming daphne. She was feeling her ancestors, she said, the Acadians who had been sent away by the English in the Grand Dérangement, the Expulsion in 1755, and wondering if they ever sat beside these bushes they had planted and wondered if anyone would remember them. Mum invited her up to the house for tea. Between sips, she told us she lived in a house on stilts where moss hung off trees like ghosts.

Normally Mum called the police about trespassers. It was a working farm, she would say, "private property," and people had no business there. Dad had just gotten his job at the plant then, in the office. There were only three cows left in the barn.

BEFORE WE WENT UP to our father's hotel room, you wanted to look around the dusty hotel lobby at the old landscape paintings and the portraits of King George and Queen Mary with ornate gilded frames. Edmund said we should go up right away. He said we should be a few minutes early. What does it matter if we're a little bit late? you said. There's never a moment to lose, replied Edmund. You shrugged. And we waited for you.

DO YOU REMEMBER HOW Cedar went on about "the universe" back when you first brought her home to meet us? She was wearing the emerald-and-diamond engagement ring you had given her, and it sparkled when she moved her hand. The universe was sending her a message: it was telling her she could fly. This was a land of resignation, she said. In Vancouver anything could happen. Here we were all so burdened. I was living at home, working in the bookstore and teaching part-time. Mum and me in the back seat giggling when you were showing Cedar around the Annapolis Valley. Cedar asking if the cows were organic. Mum told her about the accident on the garage roof, and Cedar said this could be our origin myth, that moment when I jumped and you hesitated.

She and I took a drive one afternoon before supper. Her hair was dyed the shocking pink of summer cosmos. We drove up the North Mountain to the Look-Off on the Brow of Mountain Road. Cedar stood with her eyes closed at the edge of the Mountain and chanted as she held out her arms ready to receive whatever was offered into her heart. She was thanking the universe for abundance and greatness. The sun illuminated her, and it seemed for a moment that diaphanous wings sparkled from her back. She looked over her shoulder and smiled at me. We thought of her as a flower child, Mum's words, but even when I first met Cedar, her understanding of life radiated in a way it never would in us. Cedar always had lightness, even in the darkest moments.

Later we stopped at the fire hall. You didn't want to. Mum said even though Edmund wasn't working there anymore you had to say hello to Ian, Edmund's best friend all through school. Ian was working on the fire trucks. Sunday duty, they call it. He asked how

Edmund was. You said you didn't really see Edmund much. You were busy with architecture school—that's why you were in Vancouver, after all. He looked away. You were wearing sunglasses. Ian took Cedar for a ride in the old Model T Ford fire truck, and she waved as she went by. Mum said when you got married Edmund could come home and pick you up from the church in it. You said Cedar wanted a sunrise unity ceremony on a beach on Cortes Island. Ian looked at his boots and tried not to laugh. You looked at the old fire truck when you answered. You hadn't seen him; he lived on the other side of the city.

WE TOOK THE BRASS elevator up to Dad's hotel room. I pressed my sweaty hands against the shiny walls. Edmund was usually patient with you but that day he was angry with your cavalier attitude toward time. You told him he was too serious. I tried to escape over a path of shimmering handprints. You said it didn't always pay to be first. The early bird was overrated, you proclaimed. We knocked but there was no answer. The door wasn't locked so we walked right in, Edmund first. He ran over and fell down on his knees. There were four envelopes resting on the bed. Too late, Edmund whispered, too late, his voice dry and cracking, full of ashes.

WE WERE THIRTEEN WHEN Mum made that pumpkin cake at Halloween. Dad was upstairs in their bedroom, lying on the bed in the dark. You were in the house, in the living room reading, when Nate came by to see if I wanted to go for a walk. I finished doing my chores in the barn before I crept down over the ridge to join Nate. There was one cow left. He was the first boy to kiss me, back behind the orchard, down the path. Nate loved our little old farm right in the town. He lived in the parsonage by his father's church on the small bluff by the cemetery. It overlooked the Minas Basin to the north and behind it were the Look-Off and Cape Blomidon. It was a school night and the sky was getting darker, a cool wind blowing from the north. There were only a few dry leaves left on the trees, their whispers high in the branches. Nate and I saw Mum illuminated in the window as she threw the cake across the room. The icing was bright orange.

We ran around to the front just as you came out the door and kicked the jack-o'-lantern off the top step. It flew across the lawn in pieces. The candle in the pumpkin set the brown grass on fire. Nate and I yelled for you to put it out. "Let it burn," you screamed as you came running down the steps. Edmund came out the door and pushed you aside. "We have to put it out now or it will be too late to stop it," he yelled at us. I stomped on the fiery carpet of grass in my rubber boots. I smelled

burning rubber. Edmund stomping on the flames yelling, "Run to the brook." The brook is tiny now, part
of it choked off by the condo development, but it used
to surge in the spring when the big rains came. I stood
there in the water with my hot rubber boots steaming.
Edmund and Nate dancing on the lawn, you still standing on the top step. There was a dash of moon.

Mum didn't come out after you smashed the pumpkin. Supper burned. Edmund helped her clean up,
threw out the food. She took us out to a restaurant.
Dad just stayed in the bedroom. Nobody but Nate and
Edmund talked. Nate's an accountant now. He's also in
the volunteer fire department.

I CALLED 911 AS Edmund picked you up off the floor.
He was yelling for me to get out of the room. I was
sitting on the floor next to the bedside table holding
the hotel phone. Edmund kept hollering to get out of
the room. You were in his arms. Edmund was in the
doorway screaming, "Olive, get out."

"Just a minute," I screamed back. You were throwing up in his arms.

Edmund wanted me out of the room. The 911 oper-
ator wanted me to stay on the phone. "Just a minute,"
I whispered and held the phone out to him. Edmund
was wiping the vomit off your face with his sleeve.

I dropped the phone and tripped on the gun, which flew across the room as I crawled along the floor. I was drooling on my fingers. The fire trucks arrived at the hotel and Ian came in wearing his firefighter gear. Edmund carried you to the elevator and Ian took you from there. Your arms draped over his shoulders, noises like a sick calf coming from you. I crawled after you while Edmund went back to the room.

IT HAD ONCE BEEN a grand hotel with lavish Victorian gardens. Our parents had their wedding reception in the gardens. Their wedding album was in the attic. The photos were black and white, but the splendour of the flowers was still perfectly captured in the pictures. I remember when the garden was paved over. Edmund, he was long gone, in Vancouver then. You were sailing on Aylesford Lake that summer and I was working in the town tourism office beside the concrete wishing pool directing visitors to historic sites.

WE DIDN'T HAVE A church funeral for our father, just a burial ceremony in the little graveyard near Nate's house. The trees were bare and the snow had not yet fallen. The air smelled of pine and rotting leaves. Edmund had decided on the ceremony because our

mother was in bed crying for days. You'd wanted
Dad cremated, wanted to wait until spring to scatter
his ashes. But Edmund overruled you. He said Mum
couldn't bear to put it off. You stomped about the
house. Shame and humiliation buried your anguish.
Your anger was heavy, as though you had rocks in your
pockets you couldn't remove. And your rage when you
saw the words Edmund insisted be chiselled into the
marble tombstone.

SOMETIMES WHEN I CAN'T stop thinking about what
happened, I go back to the old hotel and sit in the lobby.
The rooms have now been converted into cheap apart-
ments. The lobby is even more rundown than it was
when Dad died in the hotel room upstairs. Part of
the lobby has been turned into office and commercial space. There is a liquor store and, across from it,
a lawyer's office, a criminal lawyer. It smells of cigarette smoke from the lawyer's clients. It reminds me
of you—how harsh you became after Dad died, how
you always said it was criminals and poor people who
smoked, the dead-end types.

And you moved to Vancouver, just as everybody
seemed to do back then. You promised Mum you would
get in touch with Edmund. Cedar said you did see him
but it was only because you both bumped into Edmund

on the Downtown Eastside. Cedar said the two of you had been going to an artist's studio on the Eastside, The Church, it was called. Edmund was on the street, cigarette hanging from his lips. He smelled bad, like a garbage bag in the sun. He tried to sell you pills. "Don't you know who I am?" you yelled. Cedar had never seen Edmund, but she could tell from his eyes it was him — Atlantic blue, she said they were. Like yours. And mine.

"Just give me a minute," Edmund said, scratching at his greasy hair. Maybe Edmund was remembering when you would run behind him on the beach, always trying to catch him, and him throwing us in the air and catching us in his arms. Memories flying in his mind, wings beating so quickly they were only a blur, moments lost.

Edmund wanted you to come and meet him in a park but you said you wouldn't go there with a bunch of junkies. Cedar said Edmund wasn't suggesting that. But then Edmund said he would meet you at Kitsilano Beach. Cedar told me you guys were held up in traffic that day. Edmund was already there on the beach when you and Cedar arrived. He sat on a log by the high-water mark, looking out at the tankers. You stood by the kiosk and watched him. Cedar told you to go out to him, but you didn't. "What difference can I make now? This is not my brother," you said to her. Edmund sat for a long while and then stood up, dropping his shoulders, walking away. Maybe he thought you were late, as usual. But then assumed it was his fault, that he must have mixed up the time. He tripped and fell down on the beach. Edmund was crying. Cedar said you still didn't go out to him. Edmund got up and walked away without even brushing the sand off his face.

A month later they called. Edmund had been found in a dumpster. It was his home, the dumpster—that's what they told us, those ladies who worked with people on the street. Cardiac arrest. His heart was weak. It wasn't an overdose. It was common with heroin addicts.

After Cedar picked me up from the Vancouver airport, she took me out for coffee on the beach. I had flown out to be there for you, to fly home with you and Edmund's body. You were making Edmund's funeral arrangements on the phone with Mum so you didn't walk on the beach with Cedar and me. Cedar said she wouldn't be coming out to the funeral. I nodded, looking at the mountains. She stood at the edge of the water and lifted her arms. There was no sun that day, only mist. Cedar sang a song. It was a chant, and the words were *om* and *la la la,* and I watched the mountains vanish into the white. She held my hand as we walked back to the apartment. There was no ring on her finger anymore. Cedar told me that after she saw you ignore Edmund on the beach that day she knew she didn't want to marry you. I told her we were going to sell the family home. My mother didn't want to live there anymore. After the funeral I planned on moving to the city and getting a job. I was going to dye my hair neon blue. I still see Cedar in my mind's eye, standing at the Look-Off, the sun sparkling on the water below as she tosses her head back with such lightness.

You never knew I found the note our father left for Edmund. I didn't tell you. It wasn't like the short apology letters he left for you and me. Mum burned hers in the fireplace. I don't know what he wrote to her. But I found Edmund's, opened but abandoned, in the attic after you both had gone out west. All it said was: *The world is too much with us, late and soon*.

THE AIR WAS COOL and smelled like pine trees and sea salt on the November afternoon we buried our older brother. It was late in the day and a thin band of low red sun cut through the darkening sky. Nate's father officiated at Edmund's graveside liturgy, as he had at Dad's. Nate pulled me aside before his father began addressing the small group assembled. Nate said in a quiet voice how our father had come to sit in the graveyard, in those days before he died. We'd thought Dad was at work in the office at the plant. But he had been laid off and hadn't told us, getting ready for work every day and then driving his car to the graveyard. He parked in the back behind the church where no one could see him. But Nate had watched him from his bedroom window in the parsonage while he got ready for school, our father in his suit and holding his briefcase as he sat by the tombstones on the small bluff, looking out at the dramatic view of the mountain and water. Nate was just a boy. He couldn't have known what our father was thinking on the old marble bench by the wrought-iron gate, looking out at a horizon which for our father held only sunsets.

Our father's grave is in the corner, near the edge of the small bluff. *The world is too much with us* carved so elegantly into the grey marble. I remember staring at his tombstone as we waited for Edmund's funeral ceremony to start. Mum stood beside me with her head down and her gloved hands clasped together like two black doves.

You arrived at the last minute, standing there by the gate when they lowered Edmund into the earth. The leaves were spiralling down, stark oranges, vivid reds and yellows.

You, beside the closed gate and behind the gate, a childhood once alive with possibility, where the future soared like far-off mountains. The shovel hit the dirt. I looked up and it was the same man who had filled in our father's grave but his hair was silver now. I did not know his name. Another man took a shovel and dug into the earth. And then you, you ran forward and cried, "Just a minute, just a minute," as though one more moment could somehow make a difference. But the dirt was already falling in, leaves tumbling down like so many wings dried and turning to dust.

BACK FAT

BEING IN A SAILBOAT is like being in love. On a good day, it's the coziest, safest, and most exciting thing to be in — on a bad day it's like a coffin with standing room.

I'm sitting on the bus out to my husband, Bob, or Dr. Bob, as his patients call him, and the boat. Bob always knew he wanted to practise medicine because he liked anatomy and money. Two dudes in the seat behind me are talking about their alternative band, Nutsak, and their New Year's Eve gig in Seattle. It's early December and they're worried about Y2K, how when we fold over into 2000 it will be "game-freaking-over, man" because of a stupid computer coding error called the Millennium Bug. They fret this will spell the end of their fledgling Nutsak, their musical genius eclipsed by stupid coders, no time to make it big like Nirvana. I consider popping up over the seat and reminding them it didn't go well at all for Kurt Cobain even without any technology glitches because he shot himself and now he's dead but why bother because they would wonder what a chubby girl like me knows about grunge music anyway. I just sit there and their voices blend into the noisy chatter on the bus as we speed along to the town of Mission.

In my university department, my doctoral advisor has explained how in the early days, some programmers misunderstood the Gregorian calendar. It sounds a bit implausible but you never know. Everybody's panicking wherever you go. Maybe pandemonium will ensue. If it does, I would rather be in our cozy city apartment than trapped on a shabby old boat with constant engine problems and threadbare sails. I always need to have a plan, know what I'm going to do next. I speculate it's one of the reasons it's so easy for me to do what other people want me to. But it's harder and harder to live like this. I put on my headphones and listen to the radio on my CD Walkman. Prince is singing "1999."

Bob wants me to stay for one night to at least experience what it's like in the outstanding new marina where the boat is now moored. He's hurt I haven't made the effort to come out sooner. Three weeks ago he hired two professional sailors to move the boat from the Vancouver Marina to this place way out on the Fraser River in Mission. He wanted me to do it with him but fortunately I had exams which couldn't be rescheduled.

I was so relieved. He's been working in Mission ever since the boat was delivered, with only two short trips in to Vancouver to see me. He says it's my job to come to him. That I'll love the new location. He says it will feel like an adventure book or action movie. He says that is his favourite thing about me, my eternal sense of adventure.

All this said, the thought of sleeping on his rundown boat fills me with dread. I like *watching* adventure movies with buttered popcorn and chocolate milk. I like *reading* adventure narratives, in a soft chair with a cookie and a cup of tea. I detest real life adventure. But here I am, on the bus out to him and the boat. Every change I've ever made has been either forced on me or I've forced it on myself as a way of pleasing others. I am a master of doing what other people want, including marriage, of hunkering down and trying to endure. The adventure is trying to survive all these undertakings.

The perception from the outside is very different—I realize this. Visually, and according to my resumé, I am something I am not. There's a good hearty look to me. I'm stocky and strong. I can chop wood with an axe. I can tie knots while throwing up, hooked to a heaving boat on high seas. My outdoor skills were imposed on me by my father and my four brothers, who insisted I put in hours on the family lobster boat all the way through high school. They made me learn to sail on the weekends. They viewed all my outdoor abilities as essential life skills, not hobbies or passions. Being on a glassy, windless sea on a sunny day is lovely, but that is not a typical day on the North Atlantic.

The bus speeds along. The mid-November sun greases the thick clouds on the horizon. Dense, bulging clouds that make me pat my back fat as the orange and red blubber clouds sizzle in the glorious evening sky. My father appreciates natural beauty in the way a working man does, loving it but hardly ever mentioning it. It's a setting for hard work, not something to gawk at.

My brothers and I grew up on the North Mountain, deep in the tangled woods, in a log house with a big stone fireplace, a wood stove, solar panels, and a springfed well. There was electricity, but when the power went out, as it did in every snowstorm, we were selfsufficient. My father and my uncles built the log house together, before I was born. My uncles all live in log homes as well. My father is a fisherman, so when he isn't working on the water or at the wharf in Lupin Cove, he doesn't even want to look at the Bay of Fundy. We are distantly related to Joshua Slocum, who was born in Mount Hanley, just west of where I'm from, near Seabury Gorge. When other girls were reading *Anne of Green Gables* he made me read Slocum's 1900 memoir *Sailing Alone Around the World* about his solo circumnavigation of the globe on his trusty sloop, the

Spray. It was the original adventure book unless you count *The Odyssey*.

My father was very proud of how *all* his children learned how to haul lobster traps and use a chainsaw. That we could tie knots and stack wood. We could wildcraft medicinal plants and shuck scallops. I was happiest sitting by the fire with my mother with a piece of warm brown bread slathered in butter and strawberry jam, but I could never let my father and brothers know. The teasing would never end. My adaptation was to force myself to do everything as well as they did before retreating to the house and hearth. Only my mother understood what I was up to. She heaved a lot of sighs over the teen years and said I would eventually have to figure out both who and how I wanted to be in this world. My brothers all live near my parents. I was the only one who left.

A few passengers at the front of the bus are singing "I Saw Three Ships." It occurs to me I could take a bus anytime I want and just head wherever I want, not a destination someone else gives me. My mother would be pleased. My father? Who knows.

My father enrolled me in air cadets and I spent every summer in an air cadet camp program where we did physical training, mandatory outdoor survival courses, and studied celestial navigation. They insisted I learn to fly a plane. I was born for it, they said. My father was overjoyed when I aced my flying test. It never occurred to me I could say no. I just buckled down and endured. And yet I was still happier at home, drinking mint tea and baking with my mother. To survive the fear, I insulated myself and kept floating through life.

I gaze out the window at the glorious mountain peaks capped in sunset-stained snow. I feel nothing. Where is the splendour of nature, I wonder? I've got a letter in my knapsack which came a few weeks ago in the mail. I haven't had the heart to open this letter from Tara, or as I think of her, Back Fat. What does Tara want from me?

You can never escape childhood friends — this floats through my mind. Maybe I read it in a fortune cookie or in one of my self-help books. Maybe it was on a church sign I passed when I drove my pickup truck from Nova Scotia to Vancouver when I was twenty-five, when I was moving out west for university. Or maybe my mother said this once, not to me, but to my father, after yet another person from her past looked her up, someone who had never been her friend, and who remembered their shared childhood differently.

My mother has rheumatoid arthritis. She was late-diagnosed and can hardly use her hands now. That's the problem with letting autoimmune diseases run wild. They eat away at you until it's too late. She hid her pain from my father but not from me, when I had those cups of tea and treats with her. It was our secret and it got tucked away inside me along with her baking. My father wants me to be hale and hearty. He thought if he thrust me into a life of activity it would ward off disease. I couldn't bear to disappoint him. My mother comforted me with cupcakes.

Bob is waiting at the station, unwashed hair, rumpled clothes, bags the colour of tea under his eyes. I can smell hamburger on his breath. There's a bit of meat stuck between his teeth. No one would ever guess he was a doctor. He is the kind of doctor who does not insist on health food. The boat waits in an industrial park. I can't believe it. This is the spectacular marina? This is where he expects me to stay, even just part time? This is where I'm going to do my dissertation writing retreat?

We walk to the boat. No car. He sold it. "How can I just head out to sea if I have a car?" he says. I open my mouth and say, "back fat." I'm losing it. Bob looks at me and I say, "I mean, wonderful." I smile. Queen Positive.

We walk in silence through the industrial park, past a cedar mill. The "marina" is tucked down a steep embankment on the river, so the industry is hidden. In my mind I imagine rolling down the embankment, plopping in the water, and floating away like a log. A free log. Or a walrus.

When we walk down the dock and I see the *Snapper*, I say, "Oh, she looks fantastic," even though her paint is peeling, the teak is rotting, and the sails haven't been raised in months. It's like a mobile home at dock, I joke. Bob glares at me. I've jarred the dream. The boat is made of ferro-cement. If it can float, I think maybe anything can. I ask Bob if he's worried about Y2K. He kisses me on the cheek and says he's counting on me and my survival skills to get us through it.

It's really quiet on the dock. Like, so quiet killers could be waiting behind every pole and mast. Bob says there's one other couple living down here. He points to the boat beside us. A warm light burns deep inside. He says he's never met them but he's sure they must be friendly. Sailors are like that, he says, friendly sorts. You can count on them. Of course I think of Blackbeard and Dread Captain Ned Low, and the happy couple whose boat was hijacked in the South Pacific and who were buried in pieces on a beach on the Palmyra Atoll, written about in exquisite detail in *And the Sea Will Tell*, a crime book about an adventure gone wrong.

Yes, you can always fucking depend on the salty types. But I don't say that. Bob is so pleased with himself. He grew up on the Prairies. He doesn't know pirates are real, people coming and taking away what you treasure the most, murdering you. I want to run screaming, but instead I smile. I giggle. I feign delight.

He pats me on my cheek and gives my tit a little rub, leaving some dirt on my white jacket.

We go inside the *Snapper*. She could be a wonderful boat if she were properly taken care of. It's all toasty from a little space heater. Bob lights the kerosene lamp. It would be quaint and charming if it didn't stink so badly — the little sink is full of dishes, slimy and abandoned. I've known Bob to just throw them out and buy new ones, when company is coming. But at least it's warm. I sit down in the dimly lit salon and a dirty plate sticks to my jeans. I look around at the stacks of books all over the place, the dirty pots and pans stacked in the mahogany galley. Bob finds one clean pot and starts cooking up the broken bits from an almost-empty bag of spaghetti. I can see the moon out the little portholes, shining silver on the river, and the snow on the mountain.

The boat also reeks of mildew. It smells like mildew and diesel fuel and kerosene and rotting food and body odour. Bob says a real sailor smells just like that. It gives me the willies, because he's got big plans for the boat and me, he says. Plans and dreams so detailed I know they were made long before me, not because of me or with me, and the plans will go on after me and I know this, but I hum inside my head so I don't have to think about it. I regretted getting married the moment I started walking down the aisle.

IT WAS ONLY A few months ago that Bob suggested this new adventure, and very quickly after that, the boat had been moved and he had started work in Mission. And then he had come back into Vancouver to see me. It was a Monday night. He arrived without even a phone call. I was about to get into the bathtub as I did every evening. There was the sound of keys in the door. He came in with the mail he had picked up in the foyer and set it on the table before kissing me.

Before his new medical job he had worked at an affluent Kitsilano clinic part-time, a clinic geared toward high-powered professionals and offering evening and weekend appointments for their jet-setting patients. Bob had insisted on calling himself a "temp" even though the correct word was "locum."

He had worked in the high North, in Rankin Inlet and Churchill, before deciding he wanted to be a sailor. When he came back from his one and only sailing trip, he decided to "try out" Vancouver, where we met at a party. He didn't pay any attention to me until he heard my last name. He worshipped my famous distant Slocum cousin. Bob proposed very quickly after he saw me in action on his sail boat. He had invited me for a sail but when the winds came up he didn't seem to know what he was doing and so I took over without saying a word. We got married after a year and then he went back up north to make money to save for the big round-the-world sailing trip he wanted us to embark on.

It was "sexy medicine," he said, working with the Inuit. They appreciated him. Bob in turn appreciated the great stories he could tell at parties, how exotic they made him seem. And now this clinic outside of the city in Mission was some sort of progressive clinic, with a bunch of hippie doctors. They needed someone to fill in for them on occasional weekdays and weekends. He could start right away. It was the spice he needed. That's how Bob described it. A bit of curry. A bit of muktuk. A taste of walrus. This would be the perfect way to bring back some excitement to our lives. We could still keep the city apartment, he said. It was a reasonable compromise. This would give Bob, and me, some adventure with like-minded people. My trips out to Mission would be a retreat from the city. I grew up in the country, so it would be perfect! I could work on my dissertation. Fantastic all around! And so he accepted the job and moved the boat.

In the tub I wiggled my toes and made splashes. He had settled into a chair to sort through mail and read the paper and *Outside* magazine, which I subscribed to for research. But floating in the tub was as much time in the water as I needed at this stage in life. I had a nice bathtub caddy my mother had sent me and it was suspended over the water with a cup of herbal tea, a muffin, and a book. As long as the water didn't get too cold, it was nirvana. A pedicure would be nice too, I thought—but I didn't want Bob to know how much I would prefer a spa outing to a high seas adventure.

My dissertation is on the anthropology of adventure and the ubiquitous role it plays in society and culture. I'm fascinated by adventure magazines, books, and television, by how the content is getting more and more extreme. Everyone needs an suv now so even a trip to the grocery store will be loaded with adventure. And if you have lots of money, you can pay a Sherpa guide to haul you up Mount Everest. I read *Into Thin Air* in the bathtub and every frightening page made me love the easy life of the slob.

Bob was jabbering out in the living room about how great life was shaping up. He was so happy he had decided to stay down south at the new job in Mission and not go back up north, as much as they were pestering him. Doctor shortage, you know. Just as soon as I finished my Ph.D. we could set off, he said.

The bathwater was lukewarm now and my dissertation felt like a glacier. I felt like a walrus. And the more Bob talked, the more I felt my rolls against the hard enamel side of the tub.

Bob came in the bathroom and so I asked him, "What about the back fat?"

He was having a pee.

"Like bacon, you mean?"

"No," I said. "Like back fat. I mean back fat. On me."

"Like bacon fat? On you? On your back?"

"No. Like do I have fat on my back? Can you see it there? Do I resemble a human walrus?"

He sighed, rolled his eyes, shook a few drips and left, calling over his shoulder, "I can't stand women who are insecure about their bodies. Don't go all Barbie doll on me, okay, sweetie? You're better than that."

From the tub I could once more hear magazine pages turning in the living room as he called from the couch: "Will you come out and stay on the boat this weekend? I don't have to work so I thought we could spend the time together at the marina. You still haven't seen where she's moored. And it's a nice place to run. There's a trail along the river. You can get back into shape." He doesn't comprehend how every single outdoor adventure I've undertaken has been done with this very body.

Bob's plan is for me to commute so we don't have to be apart all the time. I can study on the boat. I can come whenever I want (when he invites me). Like the last place, up north above the treeline, where I sat alone while he worked, except when Martelle, his colleague, would have me for tea or take me to the greenhouse to look at flowers in a snowstorm, or when the three of us would have dinner.

Sometimes we went for hikes with this ravishing red-headed linguist who was working with the Grey Nuns and learning Inuktitut. Deirdre spoke a pile of languages and when she was drunk, which seemed to be most of the time, the languages all mixed together and it was hard to know what she was talking about. She was always biting her nails and chewing her lips. She was from back home, too, but from the eastern part of the Valley floor. She explained to Bob that not everyone from the East Coast knew each other. And she hadn't spent much time on the North Mountain anyway. She said it was desolate. This made me laugh because she didn't mind the tundra and frozen ice. It seems to me that desolate is a state of mind.

Bob was great at arranging for his eclectic colleagues and acquaintances who weren't working to entertain his wife. He said it was a nice little ritual we had, how when he was busy he made sure I had something fun to do as well. It was nothing more than babysitting, assuaging his guilt for always changing plans at the last minute. And keeping an eye on me. As though he thought I might slip away when he wasn't around.

But I didn't want to live on the boat part-time and take the bus to Mission. I dreaded it. My life was in the city. I hated sailing. Or rather, living in a boat like it was a trailer because Bob's sole focus now was on making some money for the round-the-world voyage.

Until then, he wouldn't have time to sail. It was nothing like my life back home. My father and brothers would be ashamed of a boat tied up, the sails rotting and the engine sitting idle. It's why I hadn't let them meet Bob. Why we married at city hall. They struggled already to accept I was a scholar living in a big city on the Pacific side of the country. Living in a boat that didn't even sail anymore would be anathema to them. They haven't yet forgiven me for eloping, my mother especially, me being the only girl and all.

This falling-apart boat has triggered all my fears. No matter how hard I try I can't please anybody. My mechanical and carpentry skills are better than Bob's but really quite basic. Bob doesn't seem to understand that. I fished on a boat. I didn't sit below. I get claustrophobic thinking about being cooped up through the winter in the *Snapper*. I haven't told him that; I've just avoided visiting him. And the one thing I've realized is that I'm most attractive to Bob when I'm avoiding him.

I've often wondered why he doesn't just quit work and go sailing again. He has stories of sailing, but those are from seven years earlier. And there are always other people in the photos he has, people who look like swarthy seamen and were likely the ones at the helm in the storms, even though he would never admit it. They must have done the real work.

He thinks because I'm from the East Coast I've got

the sea in my blood—he grew up surrounded by land, so I bring authenticity to his sailing. *The only goddamn way the sea will be in my blood is if we sink in your goddamn boat, my man.*

I remember getting out of the tub, wondering if I'd ever loved Bob. If a walrus like me could ever love anything other than polar cod and bivalves. I stayed in the tub so long my toes and fingers shrivelled. The water got cold and grey. On the way shivering down the hall I saw a single letter sitting on the small hall table. I asked Bob if there was any mail other than that. Silence. He turned the page. "No . . . not for you," he replied.

I left wet fingerprints on the envelope for me. It was from Tara back home. Good old "Back Fat." My mother must have given her my latest address again, probably assuming Tara had matured now that she was twenty-nine years old. I didn't open it. And I left it there until I threw it in my backpack before catching the bus out to Mission. My reckoning was, I might be able to steel myself enough to read it on my "retreat."

THE BOAT ROCKS GENTLY all night long. I listen to Bob snore and pull the dirty sheets closer to me—there is a vague comfort in the smell of his stale sweat, the way he farts when he sleeps. He's very consistent in this way. I lie there all night, just in case the boat breaks free and starts floating down the river. I'll be able to get Bob up in time and rescue us. The perils of sailing are real, even when moored to a dock.

I lie there breathing in the mildew and thinking about the letter from Tara shoved in my backpack. Even though I haven't opened it, the familiar guilt gropes at me when I think about burning it with a lighter. Even when I think about putting it in the garbage I feel guilty. But that letter waits for me in the bottom of my sporty backpack like an envelope full of travelling manipulation and insecurity. Tara's probably bought a non-refundable ticket and is planning on moving to Vancouver and wants to stay with me. It's like she can't leave high school behind.

Then I think about when I was seventeen with pink cheeks standing there in a strapless bra and curled hair. Tara was helping me dress before Samuel came to get me in his father's car. I'd put on hot-pink lipstick to go with the big taffeta Cinderella prom dress and black patent-leather heels. I loved that dress. I remember thinking what a hot babe I was. Until Tara started talking.

"Back fat."

"What?"

"You've got back fat."

"What do you mean, back fat?"

"Fat."

"Where?"

"Idiot. On your back. You've got fat on your back."

"I do not."

"Yes, you do. Everyone in my family has it. All the girls. But we've got perky tits. Yours sag."

Tara hauled her sweatshirt up and they might as well have been growing off her collarbone. And she was covered in back fat. Like a walrus on a rock. But I didn't have back fat and I said, "I don't have back fat."

She smirked.

"Sure you do. And saggy tits."

I was seventeen, and even if they didn't grow out of my collarbone I know they weren't sagging because I was only seventeen.

Maidenform Sweet Nothings, Denim Red Bandana Black Lace Padded Push Up, Warner's Pure Electricity Underwire, Warner's The Real McCoy Sissy Fiberfill Pointy, Bustier by Lady Marlene, Bestform Satin Underwire, Wonderbra Hello Boys. She reeled them off like we were at a square dance. Something else I grew up doing—not that Tara would have ever been caught dead square dancing. Her father was an accountant. He had a *formal education*, she liked to tell me, not like my parents, who had *vocational* training. He would never let her go to the prom with someone like Samuel, someone who was a black guy. She wanted to know if he smelled different than a white guy. I knew she had never even kissed a boy before and she knew I knew her secret.

So then Tara added: "And get the girdle pants. For the back fat."

"Girdle pants?"

"Yeah. Slim and trim. Holds in back fat. No one will know unless they grab you really hard. My grandmother gave me her girdles. No one knows I wear them. Isn't that great?"

I hated her guts, but I didn't pout that time. She could keep waiting. This is the thing about a bully — you never know how long they'll keep waiting and plotting, when they'll reappear and trip you just when you think you've found your balance.

I grinned like I was in agreement about back fat and saggy tits and continued to smile and hate her guts all the way to the prom in the car with Samuel who asked what was bothering me. When I told him, he said I shouldn't waste even a minute of my life with anyone who didn't lift me up. Then he kissed me. He smelled like aftershave — vanilla and cedar. His skin was warm. I still think about that kiss. And my back fat.

IT'S NOON AND BOB and I drink coffee and read the paper in a diner because there are no groceries on the boat. I'm taking the four o'clock bus back to the city to do some work because Bob has been beeped. He has to work the night shift tonight. He says he forgot, and I smile.

But then I'm not taking the afternoon bus because it turns out there is no bus. Bob got the time wrong. We find this out after standing at the bus stop for thirty minutes in the rain. I ignore him and look in the gutter while Bob says things like this happen, I have to be a good sport. A guy drives by, slowing down as he lowers his window and yells, "The last bus went at noon and the next one goes at seven a.m. tomorrow." The rain hits my smiling face.

Bob makes calls at the pay phone while I sit on the curb soaking up the late-November raindrops. Picking my thumbnail, I listen to him tell me his friend Pete, a doctor who works at the clinic, will pick me up and take me to a jazz concert at the high school. Bob says he'll feel better knowing I have some company for part of the evening. I won't have to be alone in a new town. I can get to know the local community. And then I can go to the boat and Bob will be back to take me out for breakfast. I say nothing. It's easier to just go with the flow. Plus I won't be able to concentrate on my dissertation in that mildewed dirty boat anyway. Bob asks me to be positive. This is my job, being positive. The cold winter rain pelts down.

I remember when I was seven years old, on a mandatory Sunday visit with my parents to family friends in a trailer court down in the Valley. My father sat there nervously counting my mother's drinks while I watched her light smoke after smoke with her curled fingers. The family friends showed slides of old people. There were no other kids and the afternoon droned on and on and on until I couldn't stand it anymore. I ran out the door and down the small street and got lost among the rectangles people called home and slid my new red coat down a white vinyl wall. In a crumpled pile on the ground, I cried and thought about my good-smelling room back home in the log house, with my neat shelves and tidy bed covered in my patchwork quilt.

That was the first time I met Samuel. He looked out a window and saw me. I remember he held up a picture in his window, a picture of a forest. Maybe it was just a bunch of trees but I saw it as a forest. When we met later, in high school, I told him I remembered the picture. He never said a word, only smiled. When my mother found me shivering on the ground that day, he wasn't in the window anymore. My mother said I had to be a polite girl or else or else or else. From then on, I hid in the backyard every Sunday until they stopped forcing me into the car. I always swore I wouldn't ever go anywhere I couldn't leave.

I'M SITTING ON THE *Snapper* looking at all the books, but I can't read them because I'm on guard duty. This industrial park where Bob has the boat tied up is the perfect setting for a horror movie. I turn the transistor radio on and it's Prince singing "1999" again. The boat rocks. A loud knock. I turn the radio off. As I stand up the lantern swings. The slightest motion rocks the *Snapper*. A man who must be Doctor Pete yells hello and I slide back the hatch.

We jump into his shiny blue Mercedes and zoom off for the high school. The jazz concert is sold out so we can't get in. He apologizes for not buying tickets in advance. He's at least fifty and I wonder if he likes babysitting his colleague's young wife. He's close to my dad's age. We go to this Chinese restaurant and I have no idea where I am except it's some built-up sprawl of a once-small town. We pass huge churches with neon crosses, fast-food restaurants, malls which seem to repeat every mile, townhouse complexes. I could never navigate my way out of here. I'm at his mercy. He's a nice guy, though, and we talk about herbal treatments and evangelical Christians, Nova Scotia, all the places Bob has worked and I've visited, and the people who look after me when Bob works, who make me tea, take me out for dinner and drinks and teach me foreign languages.

Pete walks me back to the boat, telling me it's dangerous down here at night and how it's a weird and isolated place to have a sailboat. I know it's dangerous; he doesn't need to tell me this. The light is on in the houseboat beside the *Snapper* so at least I feel a bit better, though they must be in a trance as I haven't seen a single person in or on the boat. Pete asks me if I've done a self-defence course. I say no but tell him I'm really confident. I've got padding. I've got back fat, I think. I'm a walrus with invisible tusks.

He tells me he's done Tai Chi and it has made him strong. He's as fit as a thirty-year-old. Yeah, I say. Pete looms there like a post. He can throw someone twenty feet. Can knock them down and stop their heart. Just like that. He beams at this major life achievement.

Great, I say.

He stands there grinning, saying we must get together again. I can't tell if he's just being super friendly or if he's hitting on me. I say I'll be in the city a lot for the next couple of weeks. Years and years, I think. I'm almost at my limit with all of this.

I climb aboard the boat, waving. He's still there under the dull yellow dock lights. So I open the lock, slide back the hatch and stick my head out again. He's still standing there.

"Good night," I call.

"Good night," he replies.

I pull the hatch shut and lock it. Pete doesn't move.

I turn on the radio for company and it's Prince singing *again*. Then I see the letter from Tara. It's fallen out of my backpack onto the floor. The white envelope is still unopened. Back in my pack it goes, because I don't care about her news or her requests. She's been doing this for years, finding out wherever I am and sending a letter, and asking questions and demanding I write back, which I feel compelled to do. And then inviting herself for a visit. Arriving unannounced.

Never waste time with anyone who doesn't lift you up. I think of Samuel, of how years melt away. Of how being twenty-nine-coming-up-on-thirty feels so old when it really isn't—but it isn't young either. Time is sneaky that way, how it moves along and you don't realize.

I REMEMBER THE HOT July three years ago. I flew into Kentucky from Vietnam. I'd been teaching Buddhist nuns English but I had been accepted into the Ph.D. program in Vancouver so I'd finished my contract early. The hard part was leaving Viola, my roommate, behind. She had no idea what to do with her life, so she was teaching ESL until something better came along. She just didn't want to go back to Campobello Island where her father was slowly dying. The person she was at home repulsed her. She wanted to see the world.

But I had seen enough of the world and was happy when the plane brought me back over the ocean to the U.S.A. for rest and relaxation with my friend Gail from high school. Her husband was in Moscow for the summer, learning Russian. We thought it would be a good time for a long visit. We planned to drive home together—she would visit with her family in Nova Scotia and then I would head off in my pickup truck to university in British Columbia to start my Ph.D. in cultural anthropology.

Saigon–San Francisco–Chicago–Lexington, and there was Gail, all tanned and summery. In the car she told me Tara was flying in next week. Tara was going to drive back with us. I was quiet, she was quiet, and then Gail said she was sorry—Tara had announced she was coming and had already bought a ticket. When Tara had found out I was flying in from Vietnam, she had taken a month off from her summer job in a shoe store in Toronto so she could join us. She was going to the University of Toronto and doing a commerce degree so she could be just like her dad. And she wanted to join us so it would be just like the good old days. But there were no good old days, I told Gail. She shrugged.

All the way through Kentucky–Ohio–West Virginia–Pennsylvania–New Jersey–New York–Connecticut–Massachusetts–New Hampshire–Maine–the ferry crossing of the Atlantic to Nova Scotia–the drive down Highway 101 to the town of Nolen, I remember writing in my journal:

I hate the person in the back seat.

I hate the person in the back seat.

Die Die Die.

Die Die Die.

Tara said she wished she could have my inspiration and write so much.

Gail was the only one insured to drive the car, so Tara and I were always the passengers. Whenever I wanted to sit in the back, Tara would jump in the back first. Whenever I wanted to sit in the front, she would. If we stopped for a pee break and I wanted to take a walk, she would follow me. When I read a book, Tara asked which one. She wanted to listen to commercial radio and we wanted to listen to mixed tapes. She talked incessantly about the good old days, how quickly high school went, how much she missed home and all the fun we had when we were sweet sixteen, how we were always best friends. She had seen Samuel in Toronto. He was studying biology. She never thought he'd go to university, she said. It was weird seeing him there. It made her homesick. He'd seen her and waved. She said she felt embarrassed. She never really knew him, she said. I was the one who knew everybody.

PETE IS STILL STANDING out there on the dock. It's been about ten minutes. Maybe he's meditating. Maybe he likes this macabre industrial marina. Maybe he thinks he needs to be my security guard. Or see if his colleague's lonely wife might be interested in giving him a little action because he's having an extended mid-life crisis. His black shoes like beetles outside the porthole. It hits me I know nothing about him, or what he is actually capable of. There's no phone on board and no gun. I feel a panic attack building. It's been building for a long time. My life is over.

At the table I make a plan: I'll start the boat. Right. The wheel and the throttle are outside — so I can get the boat running, but it will be tied to the dock with the engine going and us not escaping. *Us*: I'm thinking about the boat as my companion now, something I'm responsible for. The shoes are still there. I look through a drawer in the galley and pull out a knife. Armed.

Pete keeps standing there and I keep looking at his feet. And then I see that letter from Tara and think again about our road trip through the United States. At the washroom stop on the interstate, Gail had rolled her eyes. She couldn't believe the way Tara was behaving, how childish she still was. I was furious and asked why she had let her come along in the first place, which made Gail feel bad. *Sorry*. It's just that Tara never really had any friends, and it's so pathetic you can't help but pity her.

We went back outside and Tara was leaning on the car between the front and back doors. She asked me where I wanted to sit. The back, I said. That's where she was going to sit. I see, I replied. I opened the door anyway and got snug, leaning on the cooler with my feet out the window. Gail ran back to the washroom for paper towel and Tara leaned in the window and hissed, "Why do you always have to have your own way?"

I shook my head and shut my eyes. Maybe I'd get lucky and she would explode before I imploded. I don't know what happened to her grandma's girdles but she was wearing a unitard under all her clothes to slim her body, to try to keep all the bitterness and insecurity from leaking out her pores.

We stopped in Boston for the evening. Most hotels were booked so we were lucky to get a ritzy hotel room and not have to sleep in the car. Tara grabbed a bed for herself, saying Gail and I could share. Gail took a shower and came out in lacy underwear. Tara whistled and Gail frowned—even her patience finally thinning. Tara looked at me and said it was just that the two of us were too fat to wear stuff like that. But I'm not fat, I said. I remember the strain in my voice, how I wanted to yell, *If I have fat, it's my fat. Leave my fat alone.*

Nova Scotia. I was so glad to get out of the car I didn't even look at Tara. They dropped me off at my parents' house and I said farewell, breathing a sigh of relief. The relief choked up when I was in the sun at the beach two days later and Tara waddled over. I told her I was leaving for Vancouver in a few days, so I had to relax. It was a long drive. I was doing the drive alone.

That was fine with old Tara. She said she'd just sit there and read.

It was the book I'd been reading in the car on the drive up to Canada. I lay there in the sun and wished I was already heading west. And I wanted to scream, *go home go home go home* and let all my air out, but I didn't. Then she said she wouldn't mind getting a lift to Vancouver with me, taking a road trip. She didn't want to go back to Toronto. She didn't want to go back to university. She started crying. Then she wiped her nose on her arm. The snot stuck to her arm hair. I recognize lonesome when it oozes out. Then Tara said I should wear a one-piece, not a bikini. It was more flattering for someone with a body like mine. I sucked in more and wondered again if I would implode. The only place I was safe was inside my own fat body.

But right now I'm in my body stuck on this boat. Pete's still out there. The waves lap against the side of the boat and I hear the shoes click away. I peer out a porthole on the dock side and see Pete, tall and thin like Anthony Perkins in *Psycho*. He walks up the gangway and over the main wharf.

I'm alone. The clock says eleven. Ten hours until Bob's return. It's ten hours that won't end. I grab a book I need to reread for my dissertation. *The Strange Last Voyage of Donald Crowhurst*, a reconstruction of a journey, a journey of many kinds. It is based on the logbooks of Crowhurst, a competitor in the first single-handed, non-stop round-the-world sailboat race in history, the Sunday Times Golden Globe race of 1968.

Donald Crowhurst was desperate to prove himself, and very proud. He was an inexperienced sailor (as far as being prepared for zooming around the world alone), out at sea in a poorly prepared boat, the *Teignmouth Electron*. His boat was an early trimaran and should have been covered in fibreglass, but because of time pressures and delays, the plywood deck was covered with a coat of paint instead. And so at sea Crowhurst had problems with a boat that cracked and rotted and leaked. Unlike the traditional sailboat, trimarans and catamarans sit on the water rather than in it. There isn't a lot of *digging in*, and in storms one runs the constant risk of pitch-poling: running down a big wave, smashing the bow of the boat into the water and then flipping over — just like pole-vaulting, only you go upside down. And you die — a major fear of Crowhurst's. But a bigger fear of his was telling the truth. To himself. That's something I understand.

IT'S AFTER MIDNIGHT AND the boat rocks and rocks in the wind and rain. I'm in a flannel nightie, combat boots, and a leather jacket. The small heater provides a bit of warmth and a constant whir that muffles the sounds from outside.

Crowhurst was no dummy. It didn't take long for him to figure out he could never complete the journey. But Crowhurst had banked everything on winning. His business in England, Electron Utilisation, was failing. This was his chance to turn it all around. Prize money, publicity, all the opportunities awaiting the winner. So he pretended. He never left the Atlantic. He radioed in a fake course with vague positions. He kept a fake logbook and planned a rendezvous with himself when the phantom *Teignmouth Electron* sailed back into the Atlantic. Placing second or third would mean his logbook wouldn't receive the same brutal scrutiny first place would bring. If he could carry it off.

The romantic Frenchman, Bernard Moitessier, was in the lead, sailing without a two-way radio — he said it destroyed the purity of solo sailing. In letters fired from a slingshot to passing boats, Moitessier explained how he had decided, after rounding Cape Horn, that life in Europe was insane. He had no desire to return and headed to the South Pacific to spend three years on a remote atoll in the Tuamotu Archipelago.

While people were busy debating the apparent madness of Moitessier, Donald Crowhurst was actually going nuts. With Moitessier following his heart, Crowhurst was now neck and neck with Nigel Tetley, another British sailor, who was driving his boat into the waves trying to catch up to the imaginary position of Crowhurst. Tetley strained his boat too far and it sank. Now he was sitting in a dinghy at midnight, awaiting rescue.

TWO A.M. I'VE BEEN on deck four times now. Pete hasn't come back, thank god. The wind is still blowing strong and the boat keeps rocking. I try to sleep but the hideous shape of the lantern swaying sends me stomping back up on deck, convinced we are adrift. We are still at the wharf. Shining the flashlight around, I scan for perverts. Relief. The light of the neighbours still burns. I'm not really alone. So I creep off the *Snapper* and sneak up to the side of their boat. Just need to see another human, even one asleep. It's a night light. There is no one on board. I'm utterly and completely alone. It's just me and Bob's dreams, tossing from side to side.

Back in the boat, I sit on the bunk. I'm terrified and covered in sweat. I can't sleep because I've realized the boat's lower in the stern than the bow. We are sinking from the fucking stern. My heart is pounding and I'm hyperventilating. I do deep breathing. I get control. Maybe it's all in my head. Maybe we aren't sinking. I take a glass and put it on the floor. It rolls to the stern. So I rip up the cover over the diesel engine, expecting to see water flowing in. Nothing. At this point I notice the fuel injector pump is broken. The neglected engine is idle in every way. So much for escape. I hop back to the bunk, knocking over some books.

FOUR A.M. THE FATES propelled Crowhurst to the lead. His logbooks show his descent into lunacy as he realized he would be found out. Reality drove him mad. After developing his own psychotic, religious-type philosophy in logbook entries concerning mostly "the game" (which he felt he now understood), Crowhurst began a countdown and made his final entry. Then, accompanied by his broken chronometer, he jumped overboard. So much for Donald Crowhurst.

The *Teignmouth Electron* was found floating abandoned on the Atlantic, with the logbooks awaiting inspection. Crowhurst died in this bubble of crazy, but the truth cruised on, awaiting discovery.

DAWN. AS GREY LIGHT breaks on the horizon, I sigh into the now-gentle wind. I'm on deck, leaning on the mast, drinking instant coffee while wrapped in the sleeping bag. I hold an umbrella up to the soft drizzle. I can jump to the dock if we start sinking. No perverts can creep down below and surprise me. I can see the horizon. I'm steady. I've been sitting on the deck since 4:14 a.m.

Standing up, I begin to open the hatch to go below. I'm hooked to the safety line in case of an unanticipated huge gust. It's like I'm on a leash. I unhook. I realize now how this must look...how things have always looked. The adult forgets what the little kid knew and vows are betrayed until, the moment when it's clear, at some stage you can't pinpoint, you begin plotting the course of your own sorrow. Never be with anyone who doesn't lift you up, Samuel said.

Morning brings a whole new perspective. It's time to redefine adventure. To inhabit myself in my own way. And be in the world the way I am.

I go below and get dressed before climbing back on the deck with my backpack. I rip up Tara's unopened letter and chuck it in the dark water. The pieces of paper float on the waves and the current quickly pulls it all away.

MY FACE REFLECTS IN the bus window, and when I press my nose to the glass, I see the morning sunbeams and shadows marbling the road and streets and trees as we speed by en route to Vancouver. It's the same thing, people behind me and beside me going on about Y2K and the approaching End Times. But it doesn't bother me. We won't know until New Year's Day and there are a few weeks of living before then, and not a day to be wasted. I've got my CD Walkman on and the radio is playing Cher. I switch it to the CD and Emmylou Harris sings in her tremulous soprano about not knowing why she forgot to say goodbye — but I know. Sometimes you don't need to. I giggle and feel my lips against the window, my humid breath blowing back warm on my cheeks. I have survived the night. I have returned from my strange last voyage and my sturdy body is my own boat.

INSOMNIS

A CAR SCREECHES INTO her dream where she is tiny and sitting on a sunny lily pad and then she is furious and wide-smacking awake in the dark city night of her room as the car screeches and squeals away leaving rubber on the road, taking her precious and precarious sleep with it. The sheets are soaked and bits of far-off laughter float in the open window on a humid current of air, cutting through the thick summer night, coming over from Gottingen Street, from the parking lot behind the house, from yards and sidewalks, in through the window, to the woman who won't sleep between now and dawn.

The doctor supposes she has *transient* insomnia. "From moving so much?" she says. He laughs. Well, yes, from that too. But he means short-term insomnia. As opposed to *intermittent*—on and off—or *chronic*—constant—insomnia.

"But I thought it would be better when I moved home to Nova Scotia," she whispers.

"Maybe it *will* get better," he says, "maybe when it's winter, when the air is cool."

"Maybe not," she says. "It's always worse in the winter. And then it's not just insomnia—it's seasonal claustrophobia, too...winter."

He laughs. "Location, location, location...maybe you should move out of the city. Maybe you should move to a better part of the city. My diagnosis is chronic bouts of transient insomnia. Stress-induced. Go to sleep...think about moving somewhere nicer," he whispers, his finger on her nipple.

The doctor turns his head on the pillow and his lips touch her earlobe and he exhales wet breath and slowly spreads his fingers over her neck. He murmurs a story about whitewater canoeing and stars and pretty things until he snores deeply and falls into sleep with his leg across her stomach and hand sticking to her ribs. It's the fifth time he's found her late-night dancing and the first night she's brought him home.

Outside, a woman's shrill voice catches in the thick hot air: "Here, kitty-kitty." A car starts in the parking lot outside. Kitty does not come and the woman hollers again as the car backs up and then drives off. "Kitty-kitty, come in now. It's past late, Lister. Kitty, you stupid kitty, it's way past late."

The car noise fades and then it's just him snoring in her ear and then more "Lister, Lister, Mister Lister" — the lady's voice rising and stretching on each *Lister* as though Lister might be sitting in a treetop and she must throw his name up through the leaves. But outside, the cat does not come.

Inside, the snoring does not stop. She nudges the doctor awake and he snaps upright, rubs his temples. Lies back down. Pulls her to him. "You should drink less coffee," he whispers.

"It's always like this," she says. "I am a creature of the night."

"Poor you," he says. "Poor creature."

"Poor you," she says. "What about being on call and not sleeping?"

He mutters, "That's different — hospital's air-conditioned."

His breath on her neck, hands moving slowly over every curve of her body, the heat of the night melting them together, her face pushed into the damp pillow, every part of him hot inside and outside of her. His lips on her spine, pulling her hair, her head back, her hips lifting off the bed, gasping. "Shush," he whispers in her ear.

SHE SITS ON THE back deck, her naked body drying rough with salt crystals. The smell of their sweat is acrid here, where the air is cooler, but the smell is lost as the scent of the night bloomers rises from her verdant garden, the fragrant evening clematis running up a chain-link fence and sealing off this urban Eden.

The cat lady calls out again, each syllable so elongated the young woman knows her hands must be cupped like a bullhorn. The voice breaks, then stops. Far-off traffic sounds drone and laughter floats over from a neighbour's rooftop balcony. She loves the city on the hot summer nights when she cannot sleep, slipping from the confines of the house, sitting outside in the dark. The house a veritable sepulchre for the winter insomniac, the snow dampening the nighttime sounds of life, when the window can't be opened, sealed in from the cold, sealed in from the world.

SHE ALWAYS WALKS QUICKLY across the Commons. It's dangerous. She knows this. She always says *never again*, but each time she slips back, safe, into the house, she knows she will cross over again, in the dark when it's dangerous, when the night city is alive and mysterious.

She had slipped inside the house from the back deck and into a dress and sandals, pulling her hair back in a ponytail. Then quietly out the front door and down the steps, the man in her bed still asleep. The old neighbour, dark as night, sitting on his front step.

"Evenin'," he said, dragging on his cigarette. "Shouldn't be goin' out alone. You know it, girl."

She knew it. "Insomnia," she said. "Going to get a movie."

He shook his head and she walked past him, down Maynard Street.

Then she was moving fast — as she is now moving fast, halfway across the Commons, running even though there is no one around. Scared and excited. Her sandals clipping on the path. In the winter she'd be in the tub, hoping the water and candles would bring sleep. There is no traffic crossing Robie Street, but a police car drives up as she steps onto the sidewalk.

"Problem, Miss?" the cop in the passenger seat calls out the window. His head is shaved.

"No, no problem." *Shit*, she thinks. "Looking for my cat," she says. "Lister."

"Now, you know, dear, it's not safe to be out in the neighbourhood at night. Cat'll show up in the morning looking for breakfast."

Do they think she would be safer on some quiet South End street, she wonders? What they think is that they should drive her home, but she says she lives only a block away. They sit in the car with the engine purring, watching her walk up Compton Avenue. She turns around and waves at the police and then walks into someone's dark driveway. When the sound of the car fades off, she runs back out to the sidewalk and to the bright lights of Quinpool Road.

Dripping sweat at Video Difference — open twenty-four hours, for shift workers and insomniacs. She's looking for a movie to start the delta waves in her head, the brain waves which relax you and summon sleep. There is no cable in the house, not even a DVD player, only a VCR. She finds *Marathon Man*, a "retro" movie, the girl at the cash calls it. It's almost always the same girl on the graveyard shift, a girl who says she moved from the Valley to the city. Her hair is window-cleaner blue. She says she has insomnia too and when she does sleep she has nightmares about her brothers, one dead and one who may as well be. The clerk makes change while she puts a quarter in the bubble-gum machine on the counter.

She blows bubbles as she heads back across the Commons. Under the sallow lights of the park. In the east, the sky is lightening. Soon birds will chirp, traffic will roar, people will parallel park on the street in front of the house and she will be in bed with a stranger, searching for a few early morning hours of sleep before she drifts through a hot day on iced coffee and fatigue.

Her neighbour is still out smoking as she comes, gleaming with sweat under the streetlight on Maynard

Street. Home. She wipes her forehead and tightens her ponytail. This sweat is from relief, and she can smell the difference. She sees the old man from the corner. She waves as she steps from the curb, and her toes poke warm fur.

THE OLD NEIGHBOUR WATCHES her, white and sweaty and kneeling on the road by the skid marks. He hobbles over and shakes his head. They pick up the big cat together. Its head lolls, neck broken, eyeballs bulging from the sockets. She cries and he pats her shoulder.

"Poor old Lister," he says in his love voice. "Lister, my boy, you shoulda stayed in tonight...you know it, Lister, my poor old boy." He strokes the cat, fur soft as pussy willows.

"It's hard," she cries, "so hard when you can't sleep."

"It is, so it is," says the neighbour, patting her damp hand.

And they hear the lady calling again, over on Creighton Street, each syllable shooting out like gunfire, a tiny pause as she reloads with air and resumes, relentlessly now: "*Kittykittykittykittykittykitty.*" The lady is standing on her step, fat and old, wearing an orange nightie and pink slippers, her hand clutching the railing. She screams. The eastern sky is forget-me-not blue. Here, in the city, the summer morning breaks through the last film of night as the transient insomniac and the old man slowly cross the street with the slack bundle of fur and bones in their arms.

DESIRE LINES

GREETINGS AND SALUTATIONS from the mists, *my fellow wayfarer!*

That was how the email began. He was obviously still living out east, in the same place on the North Mountain. He assumed I would be happy to hear from him. He didn't use my name, but as I read on I realized this wasn't some kind of promotional email or solicitation. It was meant for me and me alone. He was in Vancouver and did I want to get together?

I wasn't expecting an email from my father. After all, I was thirty-eight years old and hadn't seen the man in thirty years. I had just biked home through Pacific Spirit Park after teaching a class at the university. The paths in the park are carefully maintained and marked, unlike the wild country trails and pathways I knew in my early childhood. It's part of what drew me to civil engineering, my interest in the paths we create as opposed to paths which are prescribed. My husband was picking up the boys from school and I'd decided to use my last bit of time at home to plod through a backlog of work correspondence.

My father asked in his email if I remembered when I lived with him at The Mists, or the magic of the North Atlantic landscape which I'd been away from for so long. *You were very young,* he wrote, *so you probably don't remember much from your early childhood. It was a long time ago. We all move on and I can see you have done so very nicely. Congratulations on your great job! I'm so proud of you.*

One fact I've learned as an adult is to never assume my children won't remember what happens. And not to assume adults can control which parts children remember. Childhood memories are like photos that have tumbled out of an album, snapshots that don't provide the complete picture. But we remember stories we've been told, and stories we've overheard. We take this information and the episodic memories we have and string together a story. Even as adults we try to complete the childhood story. We never stop trying to find the ending.

WE MOVED TO THE North Mountain the summer I was four and my mother was pregnant with my little sister, Morgaine. They had bought one hundred acres of land near Lupin Cove. My father made the house himself and we lived in a tent pitched in a meadow surrounded by forest while he built it. My mother told me this. I remember the tent was green and there was a path through the meadow to the house. I loved this path that cut through the tall grasses. In the meadow, purple vetch threaded up through the grass stems and touched my mother's round belly. The grasses grew so high they were taller than me, but I could look up and see how they touched my mother's breasts. I drew pictures on her stomach with icing coloured with beet and carrot juice. Then she'd let me lick it off. The acreage was mostly forest, except for the clearing around a large, rickety barn. They put a sandbox in the clearing where I played with my pail and shovel.

There was also a path through the woods. It was a twisting path my father had cut through the pines to the clifftop jutting out from the trees over the Bay of Fundy. He called the path "the labyrinth of life." It snaked through the forest to the perilous brink of the cliff. The path was difficult and winding, with sharp turns where you had to slow down. My father said this was the main purpose of his pathway — everyone was forced to stop hurrying and consider their journey as it unfolded. People needed to be open to sudden turns and trust the way ahead. Being in the moment would take over and time would lose meaning.

Before you knew it, you would arrive at your destination, and *le voilà*, enlightenment, or *éclaircissement*, as the French Acadians say, when you reached the bench of wisdom! Every age had an awakening, my father said, with people like him called to be its prophets, ushering in the awakening.

On a clear day you could stand at the edge of the cliff and see all the way down the bay toward Maine, which was four exhilarating hours away by boat as the crow flies or a long, boring two-day drive by car, as my father explained.

The bench at the edge of the crumbling cliff my father had made from driftwood cast to a silvery white by the elements. He encouraged us to sit on the bench and look for water nymphs and selkies. He insisted people had been spotting them in the bay for generations. They swam in with the tide, he proclaimed, as though he were a marine biologist with a peculiar specialization.

My mother's rule was we were allowed to sit on the bench only if an adult was with us. My father said my mother was too protective, she'd ruin us. Driftwood was cured by the salty bay and the wood was endowed with a strength which milled lumber did not possess. The full baptism and sculpting by the breakers and rocky beach made the wood enduring and rugged, he told us. The bench would protect us. Humans could only hope for the same combination of splendour and toughness. My father wore a long leather necklace with a tiny piece of driftwood dangling near his heart. His talisman, he called it.

I remember how excited I was when the house was finally ready — if you could call it a house. I was too young then to know my father wasn't much of a carpenter. It was tall, almost rectangular. My father, or Ocean, as he insisted everyone, including his children, call him, named it *the tree house* even though it was not near any tree, but in the centre, *the heart* of the field. He described the building as *a salute to the trees*. He believed the names of people and of objects and buildings should reflect their true nature.

My father loved talking about his quests on all sides of the continent. The high North had called him and he had journeyed to Whitehorse and onward to Utqiaġvik, which was surrounded on three sides by the Arctic Ocean. The sirens of the south then sang to him, and he journeyed to the southernmost point on the Tierra del Fuego archipelago. My father stood with his toes in the water at the end of the world where the South Pacific and the South Atlantic swirled together, where the water met the earth. Here he took his spirit name. The ocean waves had called to the eternal flow inside of him. My mother told me this story when I was a teenager, one of the few times my father's name came up.

The house Ocean had shoddily built on the commune had four stories. The woodstove and kitchen were in the cellar, from which a spiral staircase led to the first floor, where the living room was, and then the second floor, with our mother's workroom and a library. The third floor was where I slept, and the fourth floor, a loft, was where they had their bedroom with a balcony. It was in this room my mother gave birth to my sister. My father was determined she'd have a homebirth and apologized to me that I was born in the hospital and not on the land as Morgaine was.

We buried the placenta together in the field. The maroon flesh quivered as my father placed it in the hole we'd dug. It was covered in a grid of arteries, the cord attached in the centre, an alien topography, a map to the secret of life. The organ glistened as the sun fell on it before we covered it in handfuls of earth. A woman's body is miraculous, Ocean said. He patted my tummy as he said I too would one day create a miracle.

Morgaine slept with my parents for the first two years, constantly breastfeeding. The baby, as we still called her then, started waking up crying when they would burn incense and massage each other.

This is when they moved her into my room. Morgaine continued to wake up in the night and would crawl into bed with me. Sometimes I wonder if I remember correctly. We never had normal bedtimes, sometimes rising and setting with the sun and just as often staying up late into the night for Solstice or other High Holy Days, as my father called them.

By day Morgaine was a chatterbox. At night she was quiet as we listened to coyote howls, the wind rushing through the trees. Then to the sounds of chanting and drumming once my parents started having people come and build on the other parts of the land to join the Community. My mother would put us to bed, but if we got up and ran outside, my father would tell her to let us be. We would watch the vesper bats dart through the twilight. We helped our father build bat houses.

One day we heard the crows screaming in the trees, two of their babies on the ground below a nest. Ocean left the dead one to nature and took the injured fledgling to the barn where he fixed its damaged wing. When it was able to fly, he released it for the crow family in the trees to reclaim. But the bird had imprinted on my father by then and would soar down when he'd throw some scraps. It would perch on his arm.

Ocean came home with a large tattoo of a crow on his forearm. "A murder of crows, Eve, although that word masks their wisdom, their humour, their loyalty and kindness," he said as he showed me, black ink on red and puffy skin.

Morgaine was repulsed by the diet of crows. "Yucky. They eat garbage and dead stuff."

Even though she was disgusted by how the crow pecked away at roadkill, the bird seemed to like her, never hopping away as it did from me.

"A part of the life cycle, Morgaine," our father told her as he picked her up and swung her to his shoulders. "You see, the crow is prehistoric. It will be here long after we're gone."

Ocean told us people were scarring the earth, that one civilization after another had been wiped out because of arrogance, a sense of invincibility, forcing the ways of men and progress on the land. But nature would only tolerate so much. He'd explain how vaccinations were creating legions of zombie children, implanting illnesses, making us vulnerable to the coming plague.

To the west of the bench by the perilous cliff was an old abandoned graveyard with toppled tombstones, people who'd died of the Spanish flu. It was a flu they caught in reaction to the First World War, Ocean said, their immune systems weakened by the horrors inflicted on humanity by powermongers.

"And look at what's happening in Lebanon now. The poor Palestinians. It's a mess, Apsara."

Apsara was what he called my mother, Sanskrit for *celestial nymph*. She would step in when he ranted, interrupting him with talk about her herb garden. She was growing meadowsweet and valerian and lemon balm.

She planted sea buckthorn and it was growing stead-ily, covered in brilliant orange berries from autumn into winter. The garden was small at first but after a few years my mother expanded it. It thrived with her careful attention and by the time I was six the garden was thick and lush. When I came home from school Morgaine and I would play, chasing each other over the paths through the garden, our footsteps releasing scent from the aromatic creeping thyme which grew in between the stepping stones.

My father wanted me homeschooled, and my mother wanted me at school. Ocean said school would brain-wash us. And when the winter weather blew, we might freeze to death waiting for the school bus on the dirt road. It was then she had started to grow weary, the sleepless nights and constant tending to little children layered in with the endless cooking and gardening, and my father's ceaseless ideas. She knew she would be the homeschooler, not Ocean. We didn't even have a globe because my father felt it would give us a limited sense of the world. He would hold up his hands and say the earth was an endless expanse. We were pure energy.

Sometimes, but not very often, he'd take us to see his mother when he went down the Mountain to town for groceries. My father usually left shopping to my mother, but sometimes she'd complain of a headache and he'd pack us in the truck. Grammy would stand in her apron on the steps of her old house, hands on her hips, telling him he should get a real job, how he was being ridiculous. He stopped bringing us down to see her. She wanted to take us to church on Christmas Eve. He called that "Yule." He liked the Easter Bunny more than the crucifix. He was all for fertility, he said.

Our mother read us fairy tales from books our grandmother had given us as "Yule" presents. They had been our father's childhood books. He did not approve of his old books. If he came in when she was reading to us at bedtime, he would stand with his arms crossed.

"*Tut, tut.* Apsara, you're filling their heads with stories designed to make children afraid of the woods rather than feel at home there. They're stories engineered to rob children of their innate ability to connect with nature."

At first my mother would just wait for him to finish preaching and he would eventually go outside.

When he started taking the book out of her hands and gently closing it, she stopped reading to us. We cried and Ocean pointed at us and clucked that this was exactly what he was talking about—our mother had filled us with needless fright. He took over our bedtime stories then. Ocean told us about animal spirits and magical beings. And his plans for the property. He had started to convert the old barn. All he needed was money, he said. The universe would provide. Morgaine snuggled in his lap and dangled on his every word as he stroked her hair. She would reach up and play with the driftwood talisman hanging by his collarbone.

MY MOTHER GOT A nursing job down in the Valley at the hospital. Although Ocean had been happy when she'd originally abandoned her career to join him as his muse on his mystical journey, now he was thrilled she was bringing in money. When we did career day in school, he told me he was a currency trader. I thought this had something to do with ocean swells, but never asked about it for fear I would sound silly. He was working on a computer program that would make us rich. Apsara could do her part now.

"Like I haven't been doing it all along," she snapped back at him.

While having children had made my father more of a child himself, what he called a *free spirit*, it had made our mother more cautious and protective. He would send us out to play and she would come out and tell us where it was safe to play.

My father was pleased with how my mother understood how to interact with a variety of people in what he called "the mainstream world." They all loved her and no one treated her like "a flake," as they treated him. She could infiltrate linear society. She could move in all worlds, with no barriers. He wasn't able to do it with the same ease, he said. She'd roll her eyes at this and sigh. By then she was reluctantly living at The Mists, as most people called it. My father had decided to call the property "The Mists of Avalon" when he was looking for people to join. He got the name from the title of a recently published novel my mother was reading. She told him it was a reinterpretation of Celtic myth, from a female perspective, and that if he had read it he would know it was not the right name for the property. But my father insisted it was the perfect name. He didn't need to read the book. Ocean knew what was in it without even seeing the words.

By then, there were people camping on the property and building their own huts in the woods. Nova Scotia was a spiritual siren, my father said. It called to their souls. There was a young woman named Wildflower, with braids and a man named Fern and his friend Spruce. And Spruce had a girlfriend named Evening Star. And more came, all with nature names, some with Sanskrit names. They did yoga and meditated and chanted and drummed. There was an architect whose wife had died in a car accident. "Transitioned," they called it. He helped my father with expansion plans. He would winter in Lesbos and come to The Mists of Avalon in the spring. He was originally from Malta and found the Nova Scotia winters too harsh.

Without even asking, they replaced my mother's small garden with a huge herb garden in the shape of a Celtic cross. My mother just shrugged. She didn't even weed it anymore, so she was relieved to have someone else claim the garden. Ocean had someone fly over and take an aerial picture. He put it in a brochure to advertise the property and more visitors found us. *Eco-travellers*, he called them. *Spirit travellers. Sojourners in The Mists.* The old barn had been fully converted now. My mother was permanent staff at the hospital by then and her entire salary was going into The Mists. There must have been thirty people living there at this time in various small buildings and yurts.

My father would make me big bowls of oatmeal with ground flax and maple syrup. Syrup making was a community event, everyone carrying their pails of sap from all over the property to the cookhouse. We'd have a sugar shack and make buckwheat pancakes and maple syrup candy. And in the other seasons, we'd have the amber syrup to remember the trees' blood.

My father would hold my hand and walk me to the end of the driveway on school days when my mother was at work. He'd make shadow puppets with his hands. We'd pretend to be dragons when the air was cold and our breath was steamy. He'd leave Morgaine sleeping in the house. She never liked to get up early.

"Your mother worries too much. When an adult

worries, a child worries, Eve," Ocean advised me. Sometimes he would carry me on his shoulders and I felt like a tall prehistoric bird that had known the crows back when the world was new.

During the day Ocean would look after Morgaine, if you could call it that. When I came home she'd show me the rye bread they'd made, or the pictures they'd painted, or the dream catchers they'd woven. He would take her to the beach to harvest kelp, and they would prepare a stew that made the house reek. But often she just played by herself all day. Even as a very young child she was able to spend her day playing with toys and invisible friends. Morgaine said Wildflower came over to clean the house and do laundry. When I'd come home on the bus, usually it was just Morgaine waiting, her hands clasped together by her heart like a little priestess. The kids on the bus called us the hippie people who lived in a cult. I had just turned eight and remember being self-conscious in a way I had not been the year before.

Sometimes my father left me alone to wait for the bus. I was terrified to wait there. Across the road was a thick forest and I was sure I heard unearthly things in the trees. The woods on our property were familiar, I told myself. They were safe and rang with birdsong. But I didn't know what lurked across the road. I never told my father. I didn't want him to think I was afraid.

One morning my mother came home sick from an early shift. She'd turned around at the hospital and driven right back. I was waiting alone for the bus. The coyotes next door had killed the neighbours' sheep. Now they had two Great Pyrenees dogs on the property to guard the new flock. My mother was terrified of the enormous white dogs. I wondered if this was what lurked in the forest across the road but I still didn't say a word to my father. I remember how Ocean had started yelling at my mother around then, about how she had to get in touch with her heritage.

She had black hair, like Morgaine. My father said it was their Indian blood, that the Native peoples out there on the Pacific were holy and she should tap into the power—it was nothing to be embarrassed about.

She rolled her eyes. It was just an old family story he wanted to believe.

He would pick Morgaine up and call her his Indian princess. I had blue eyes like him.

My mother started getting a ride to the Valley with a neighbour so my father could have the car at home. This way he would have no reason to make us walk so far to catch the bus in nasty weather. When the weather was bad, she started staying down in the Valley, in town at a friend's house, a friend she worked with.

It wasn't long after that she told Ocean she was going on a maternity leave. It was early spring. She said she'd be staying down in the Valley permanently. Ocean was convinced she'd been contaminated by self-indulgence. But then my mother told him about what he called the "sacred breech" — the baby belonged to the friend she was spending the nights with, a man who worked at the hospital with her, a doctor. He didn't live on a reserve, but he was Indigenous. That he lived in town seemed to bother my father the most.

"That's how it is, *George*," my mother said, using our father's real name like a swear word.

We could hear him crying up on the top floor of the tree house. We could even hear him crying all the way through the woods on the meditation bench perched by the dangerous cliff, howling into the wind and salty spray, wailing down toward the jagged rocks where the ocean smashed against the cliffside far below, the mists blowing in through the trees and carrying his weeping to us.

My mother said it was our opportunity for a solid life with a tangible future. The Mists would never be anything more than a run-down idea, his computer program would never be finished, and we wouldn't know how to function in the real world. Besides, our father had Wildflower.

My mother got custody of us and she decided we would live with her during the week and spend weekends with our father. She packed up, taking us but not

her sandals and her hippie dresses, nor her beaded neck-
laces and patchouli oil, her Tibetan singing bowl and her
gong. She left all her glass jars with dried herbs. And the
strewing herbs tied with string and hanging from the
rafters—the lavender, sage, rosemary, and meadowsweet. The vestiges of Apsara, she said. From then on,
she would only answer to Matilda, her real name.

We had to share a bedroom in our house in town,
in the Valley, but it was big enough for two single beds.
She bought us Cabbage Patch dolls and Barbies and My
Little Ponies. We had a Lite-Brite set and an Easy Bake
Oven. She took us for supper with our grandmother
every Sunday. Morgaine became very quiet, and she
would climb trees and hide in the high branches until
my mother would find her and send me up to bring
her down. My sister could climb effortlessly, even with
tears on her cheeks.

For all his sobbing, my father carried on as though
our mother had never even been there. Wildflower
moved into the tree house. Ocean said that to everything there was a season and love had many seasons.
We were forging reality at the forge of life, stoking our
fires, and moulding and bending our paths, pounding,
shaping, and polishing, and then casting once more
into the embers, reshaping yet again.

Our mother was into material comforts, Ocean
said, despite her heritage. It was an affliction which had

taken hold of society. She was a woman, and women were more vulnerable to material wants. This enraged her. And even then I doubted his logic, endlessly circuitous and never debatable. No matter what happened, you could put it off on the universe. It was meant to be out of your hands. Quitting midstream was hearing the call of another path. Changing paths was merely answering the calling, not lacking the tenacity to stay the course. My father had retained the same sense of wonder children had. He would try anything. He was not afraid of eccentricity. He was not afraid of the edge.

Looking back, it's easier to understand why my mother wasn't more concerned with our weekend visits. She was exhausted. She worked through most of her pregnancy. All through my twenties I hated her, no matter how my stepfather tried to explain things. Then I blamed him as well.

At first we did see Ocean every weekend, but he was busier than ever. My father lugged an enormous telescope to the balcony and we saw the North Star and the constellations, Orion's Belt, the Big Dipper, the Milky Way. Later that summer he showed us the Perseids. He thought nothing of getting us up in the middle of the night or before dawn to see a celestial sensation.

When he'd go off on "business" he had to attend to, he would leave us with Wildflower as the babysitter.

"If her mother finds out they're left alone she won't

let them come anymore," our father said. "So you stay with them."

If Wildflower was away, he brought us with him wherever he went and if he felt it was too sexy or too hedonistic and might get back to my mother, he would send us off to play. "But stay within calling distance," he said. "That's the only thing I insist on, my only commandment." And when Ocean and Wildflower were upstairs in the loft, with their drums and incense and beeswax candles, he'd send us outside to play. But he never bothered calling us to see if we had obeyed his one commandment.

At the outdoor bonfires we would sleep in the grass and he'd bring mats and blankets for us. Morgaine could fall asleep, but I'd lie there listening to them sing and chant. In the house, sometimes Morgaine would have bad dreams, and our father would appear wearing an old silk kimono as a bathrobe, smelling of salt and sandalwood, slick with sweat, Wildflower's giggles trailing in behind him.

I remember finding it odd when Morgaine was no longer afraid of the crows and began to feed them. My father's crow in particular seemed attached to her, so much so it unnerved even him. At that time I thought Ocean was afraid for her but later, when I'd think of his voice, how quickly he would tell her to leave the birds alone, I realized he was jealous. He was king of the birds. He was the one who could speak to them.

When she kept it up, he gave her a talking to. Did she want to stop coming on the weekends?

Morgaine had clasped her hands behind her back and put her head down, chastised. That was the last thing she wanted. The bird still would perch near her but she would not acknowledge it, not when our father was around. When it was just the two of us, Morgaine would wave her arms at the bird in greeting. The crow would dip its beak and caw until she croaked back at it.

At our new home in town I played with other children and spent time in my room with my drawing and paint sets, making imaginary maps for make-believe kingdoms. The four years between us seemed an abyss, with Morgaine standing on the other side. She would trail about behind me. Occasionally I would play with her and let her order me around. She liked to play "blindfold" with my mother's abandoned scarves when we were at The Mists. She even brought one to our new house in town.

"Guess what flower this is?" she'd whisper, holding the petals to my nose.

I felt sorry for Morgaine when we were with our father, how there were no other young children her age at The Mists. There were only babies and pregnant women. We were the oldest. To make Morgaine happy when we were there, I played tag and hide-and-seek with her, and all the games with elaborate rules and rituals she had made up.

At summer's close, things changed. Our father forgot we might report back to our mother. He often did not come home at night. He'd stay in another hut. He'd tell Wildflower love was boundless. We wandered in the woods playing hide-and-seek and kick the can while Ocean took pilgrims on spiritual walks and quests in the woods. And sometimes he'd go away on trips and we'd be with Wildflower for the whole weekend.

"Your father is a mystic," she would tell us at bedtime. Wildflower was twenty-two years old but she seemed much older to me then. She would whisper to us, as though she were imparting secrets about our father.

He can bend things with his will.
Ocean is able to hear the beat of his own heart
and walk in its rhythm.
He is busy stretching his soul
through the universe.

WHEN SCHOOL STARTED AND my mother's due date approached, she wanted us at home with her and my stepfather. She got very clingy and only let us see Ocean on alternating weekends. She had us help her with the baby's room, picking out wallpaper with ducks and ducklings and golden suns with smiles and dancing feet. She would burst into tears, and she would fall asleep as she read us bedtime stories. My stepfather took over the bedtime ritual. We lived in his house in town, with a big backyard, and he'd take us to the library when my mother's feet were too swollen to walk. He registered me in hockey and coached the team. My mother bought me a pink helmet.

But Morgaine always missed the meadows and woods of The Mists. She chanted in her bedroom. Sometimes my mother heard the drone of Morgaine's voice and she'd tell her to stop. She wanted her to forget. "You live in the Valley now," we reminded Morgaine. "You don't live up there on the Mountain anymore."

My mother took an old feather away from her, saying it was full of bird parasites. She didn't notice how Morgaine's face collapsed.

The baby was due any day, and we went to see our father for the weekend. It was a Friday evening. Ocean was having a harvest ceremony. Thick, chilly dew fell down in the twilight. After supper we went to "the temple" in the converted barn. People had come from all over and the upper field was full of cars and hippie vans. My father led a smudging ceremony. Then they danced, the women swirling scarves above their heads. We spun in circles with them, but when they sat down cross-legged to chant and began to smoke the sacred herb and eat little mushrooms, we got bored. We slipped outside and no one noticed. We walked through the barn door and climbed down the stairs in bare feet. The fire circle was prepared, the great logs standing upright, ready to be lit aflame.

It was evening but still so bright with the harvest moon rising. Morgaine wanted to play blindfold. She wrapped the scarf around my face. I tightened it and Morgaine pulled the silk even more. It hurt my eyes. She took my cold hand in her sweaty little one, the palm so meaty, and led me into the trees. The pine needles were cool and sharp under my feet. At first I was worried she was taking me through the labyrinth to the cliff. But Morgaine just guided me straight ahead, bringing me low to dodge the odd branch. But then I could feel the mist on my skin. The air was tangy. The silk blindfold was damp and I heard the waves crashing below. She had bypassed the labyrinth path, taking us straight through the woods to the bench by the edge of the cliff.

I let go of Morgaine's hand and pulled at the blindfold, but it was so tight. Finally I hauled it down. I did not see Morgaine, only the crow.

The bird was there.

The bird flies into the mists.

This is what I remember.

And then I saw her ahead of me by a tree, and the bird was by the tree. There was sky above the mists, sunset sky like a strip of ribbon, but the wind was picking up, the mist expanding.

I heard Morgaine cry out.

Or perhaps it was the crow cawing. She looked up and the bird was there in the sky. I glanced back down at her.

"Come away from the cliff, Morgaine!" I yelled at her, I am sure of it. I told her only birds can fly, that she should come away. How she'd tricked me.

I ran through the woods with the branches tearing at my face. I was at the fire, my cheeks streaked with tears and blood. When I saw them, I stood hypnotized as they danced and howled at the full moon, which hung low over the meadow. I called to them but they were gathered around the fire, faces ageless in the flickering orange flames, swaying to the bongo drums, murmuring, the woodsmoke mingling with the mists. They thought I was part of the ritual. My father kept drumming on, smiling at me.

Finally, it was Wildflower who saw I was not singing but crying and pointing toward the water, toward the cliff. And she went running. Then Ocean put his drum down and ran after her. But it was already too late.

YEARS LATER, IN VANCOUVER, the city where my mother was born, I was talking with my husband, who was at that point a psychology student. While it was rare for me to even mention my sister, I relentlessly interrogated my own memories. My husband always said I was not haunted by my memories — my memories were haunted by me, trying to understand what really happened that night. He said sleep deprivation was used as a form of torture — it distorts and reshapes memory. We never slept properly at The Mists, in the house or sleeping on mats in the meadow. We had no consistent bedtime or wake-up time. It was easy to think a dream was real, that the crow had perched on Morgaine's shoulder croaking an ancient song.

"With the mists you couldn't have known how close to the edge she was, Eve," my husband repeated.

As an adult, I knew this. But when it happened I was only an eight-year-old child. And even at eight, our minds are not always able to form detailed memories. We have barely begun to encode memory at that time — what my husband calls "memory rehearsal."

"Childhood amnesia is what causes many adults to have trouble recalling complex memories and events which occur before the age of ten," he explained. "Especially with trauma."

The adults at the fire were high, and they were

drumming and singing and chanting — they paid no attention to us. This is the truth.

When I was finally finishing my Ph.D. in civil engineering, I talked to an ornithologist from the biology department at a campus event and she assured me a crow would not imprint on a child, and certainly would not switch loyalties: the crow would be forever faithful to the adult who raised it.

I REMEMBER LEAVING IN the back of a police car. There was a helicopter. They had to search the water. My mother was in the hospital having the baby and there were problems, they said. She had to stay in longer. Later, I found out they had kept her there, under observation. She had postpartum depression on top of it all. She was flooded with hormones and grief, but she held my little brother to her breast.

My stepfather's auntie took me to the city on the day of the funeral and we went to the Discovery Centre and took a ferry ride across Halifax Harbour to Dartmouth. She called it "the big city," and it was to me — the first time I left the countryside. She kept me with her for a few days and when the first snow of the year came down she bought me a pair of snow pants and took me snowshoeing

And life returned to normal, as it does. The days

got very short, and then they got longer. I refused to visit my father again. As far as I know, he made no effort to see me. I would walk to school and back, and my stepfather would take me to the hockey rink. My mother stayed home with the baby and didn't go back to work until he was in school. My little brother looked so much more like my father than he did my mother or my stepfather. But it might have been the way I studied him, looking for Morgaine but never finding her. I called my stepfather "Papa," as my brother did. Papa said Ocean was right about one thing—life was full of mystery and things happen with no explanation. We couldn't argue that one.

My mother never discussed what happened. There was a picture of Morgaine on her dresser in a silver frame, but we never mentioned it or looked at it when she was in the room. My stepfather said my mother was always trying to do the right thing, always trying to please others and never herself. She finally learned that life was a fine and ever-changing dance to keep everybody in the circle. My stepfather wasn't one who talked a lot, so when he did, we listened.

AND THEN THIS EMAIL from my father, all these years later. He said he had heard on Facebook about a prestigious park I was designing. It was curious he was on

Facebook—that social media wasn't something he thought was part of the Big Conspiracy, like vaccinations. He was already in Vancouver for the conference, he wrote, and wanted to see me before he left in a few days. Maybe we could go for a walk on the beach, he suggested.

It pissed me off that my father gave me so little notice and clearly assumed I would drop everything to stroll along the beach with him. My husband, who was now a psychologist, encouraged me to see him. "He's getting old, Eve," he said. "You'll regret it if this is your only chance."

His email signature listed a website—The Mists of Avalon—and I clicked through on the link to prepare myself for our meeting. He'd started the site, no doubt with great excitement, but now it seemed rudimentary and out of date. There was a photo of him by a birch tree looking exactly as I remembered, with long blond hair and a tie-dye T-shirt with a black peace sign. And of course, his crow tattoo on his muscled arm. It was a photo from a long time ago, from when I was a young girl.

We met at Jericho Beach. I didn't recognize him until I heard someone calling my name. My father was balding. It happens to lots of men so I should have expected it. Why I thought he was going to look like that old photo I'm not sure. I guess he'd remained the same in my mind and heart, where time moved at a different pace. My father was very thin. He wasn't tall anymore. He stooped, in the way that happens to us all. His skin was blotchy and jaundiced but he still strode along with that little smile on his face, as though he knew something no one else did, as though he possessed an important piece of information, the secret, which would bring us all together, which would unite us with the natural world, with ourselves. He had swapped out his driftwood talisman for a piece of jade on a sterling-silver chain.

He gave me a big hug, as though we had been close all through these long years. I couldn't help but stiffen. He didn't seem to notice, or if he did, he didn't let on. But I took a step back and he didn't try to hug me again. We sat on a bench and he gave me space. He wanted to see pictures of his grandchildren. I dug through my purse. He smiled when I said he could keep the photographs.

I asked Ocean what he was up to these days. I didn't mention The Mists. He was developing an algorithm, he said, a computer program, which would help him with currency trading, and he was going to make a fortune. Ocean wanted me to invest. He'd raised me right, he said. I was such a successful businesswoman.

"That sounds like a pyramid scheme, what you're describing."

He told me about the Rosicrucians, how they knew ancient secrets. Math was a language of the mystics.

We stood up and walked slowly along the beach. I asked if he knew how Wildflower was.

She was still at The Mists. She had her own house, another tall, slim house with four floors and a telescope on the top. She did the bookkeeping for The Mists and worked as an office manager in town as well. Sometimes men lived with her in the summer, but she mostly kept to herself. She had a child who was grown now, who came to visit. But she still believed in The Mists, the potential, the energy connected to its latitudinal and longitudinal coordinates. They had studied Al-Khwārizmī's medieval *Book of the Description of the Earth*. Surely I understood all this, being an expert in this field?

I didn't roll my eyes, nor did I express any sort of wonder. He didn't seem surprised.

My father coughed and we stopped and sat on another bench so he could catch his breath. I asked him if he was sick and he said he was infected with some sort of fungus in his liver but he was taking a natural protocol to heal himself. I didn't ask him what the protocol was.

"Why do you think she fell?" is what I asked.

My husband had said the same thing as my father did—Morgaine simply got too close to the edge, as children will do. Morgaine was playing bird in the wrong location. Nothing more.

And she should have been supervised by adults, my husband had repeated over and over.

My father had named the old bench after her. Morgaine's Bench. So people could sit there and remember her.

"I have a lot of regrets," I told my father.

He said people can't live with regret. It poisons them. Everyone makes mistakes. We have to carry onward. Ocean said we were all sojourners here on the earth. Each one of us is a wayfarer.

My mother had frightened us into staying away from the cliff, my father said. He had thought about it for years, and if she had not frightened us we would have had a natural caution and care. Morgaine would have taken instinctual precautions and she never would have followed a bird into the fog. He was quiet and then said neither Morgaine nor I had ever learned the right way to understand fairy tales.

But I don't think this is true.

I'd talked with my husband about how Morgaine had held my hand and how we did not take the twisting path through the pines my father had created. She'd led me straight on her own path and I was disoriented with the blindfold. Her path led straight to the disintegrating precipice.

In civil engineering we talk about the paths of desire that pedestrians take. People wear down pathways through grass when they take shortcuts, veering away from sidewalks for the most direct routes to their destinations. The desire lines. It's instinctive, this desire to take the most expedient path, not the prescribed one. Planners learn from these behaviours and try to design better pathways accordingly. Sometimes we even wait and see exactly where people have trampled the grass down, to determine the best places to lay walking paths, or the places we need to erect signs and barriers to keep people from veering off the official route. I've never forgotten the path through the meadow or the path through the woods my father believed no one would ever bypass, his belief that none of his children would deviate from his sacred trail.

My father said he had always been afraid of heights. It's why he had never put any sort of trail or staircase down to the beach. It's why he had a winding path through the trees, so he could compose himself before coming to that crazy plummet at the edge of the woods. Living in the tree house, which was really just a house with several stories, was as much as he could manage. He wasn't into extreme sports, he said. He didn't know how to rappel. There was nothing he could have done anyway, after she hit her head on the rocks. And the tide was in, so she would have drowned before they could reach her. Spirits choose how long they will inhabit the vessel we call a body. It's just harder for us to accept that what we see as children are spirit forms in human flesh. She had already transitioned into the great energy plain when they found her. We create our reality, Ocean said, even as children.

He hoped I hadn't been blaming myself, because blame was a waste of life force. My father said we must live with the eyes of a child, because it is the only way to truly live. We can never know the answers of infinity.

I didn't say anything at first. How do you respond to something like that? Then I said, with more force than I was expecting, "I do know I was only eight."

Ocean's eyes got watery and then he said he had to go meet a friend. He went off, striding down the beach now that he had rested, the sun shining on his bald head. It wasn't raining, for once, in that rainforest of a city.

I still think about my father when I look at the mountains here.

And I see her still, Morgaine, at the edge of the ragged cliff by the splintered driftwood bench, her arms out, thrusting up and down. I see her lifting off, hear the flap of her wings and the harsh caw of the crow as black feathers disappear into the mists.

BEYOND ALL THINGS
IS THE SEA

BIRDIE SAYS TO GO tits to the wind.

And I am going tits to the wind.

When the utility van whips around the corner, I crash from one hard side of the vehicle to the other, Birdie at the wheel, yelling too late, "Brace yourself, girls!" I am ripping off my poufed wedding dress when Birdie makes the turn. The wheels lift up for a second and bits of lace fly through the air. The van tires smash down hard on the road and throw me again.

I don't crash forward. Somehow, I flip in the air and smash my back against the metal wall of the van. My whole life has been about crashing backwards, an effort to exist in perpetual motion. I live for the thrill of the bolt. It's the only way I can throw off the past. Cast away what I don't understand, run from a life which has felt like a tunnel collapsing on me.

An hour to the airport. The flight is leaving in an

hour. I look at Elizabeth sitting across from me, trying to grab the round black suitcase on the floor by her feet. It sailed to the other side of the van, too, when Birdie took that last turn. Birdie and Elizabeth, the Bail-out Squad. And I know that it's the last bail-out.

BIRDIE AND ELIZABETH WERE my childhood friends, my best friends all through high school before I went to university where I almost finished my master's—classical studies. I enjoyed the Greeks and Romans. The classical studies department was located in a series of grey Victorian houses that ran along a quiet street with huge, sweeping trees. I still don't know the name of the trees. There is oblivion in the blur, a relief in the skewering of the everyday, keeping truth distorted so there is no worry of ever really seeing it.

My need to move my anxious feet first became urgent when I was reading Seneca's *Letters from a Stoic*. It was as though Seneca himself appeared behind the kindly professor at his desk who was holding forth on my thesis. An antique glass paperweight sat atop the stack of paper which was my graduate work. The same kind of paperweight that my mother had made me sell to disgusting Mr. Burgess at his antique shop. The glass twinkled in the sunlight.

The past found me there and it was unbearable. It

was time to dash. It seemed like a hallucination, a voice speaking which I alone heard: *Wild animals run from the dangers they actually see, and once they have escaped them worry no more. We however are tormented alike by what is past and what is to come...*

The professor was a cloud of frizzy grey hair and a soft English accent. Behind him Seneca appeared like a stray cherub, a rotund man in a toga. He was there before me, hovering a bit to the left like the great Gazoo, the tiny wizard in *The Flintstones*. At first I thought I might still be drunk—it had been a long, late night drinking at the Seahorse. Only I could hear him as he began a recitation. *But nothing will help quite so much as just keeping quiet, talking with other people as little as possible, with yourself as much as possible. For conversation has a kind of charm about it, an insinuating and insidious something that elicits secrets from us just like love or liquor.* Letter CV—the Roman numeral for 105. I knew it. *Epistulae Morales ad Lucilium.* Seneca's moral advice to the young Lucilius. I had read the book over and over again the previous year.

I blinked and Seneca was gone. My professor too. I was alone in my mind's eye. In the ramshackle Victorian house at the edge of the Mountain, the house my mother had inherited from an old spinster great-aunt. But not the rare antiques inside. Long-lost relatives who *did* inherit the antiques but who were never located by the lawyer. Surrounded by wealth we couldn't touch. Encircled by the tower of bills and collection notices. Relentless phone calls. We would lose the house. Nowhere to go. Haggard mother with red eyes sending her daughter with antique paperweight to antique dealer. *Do whatever he asks. He'll give you the best price. Do whatever he asks, Seraphina.*

I did.

I bolted out of the gentle professor's office. I vamoosed down to the harbour. I scampered along the waterfront watching container ships. My heart was pounding. The past was creeping from the Valley to the peninsula, finding me in the harbour city. I flashed up the hill and fled home. Panting, out of breath, going so fast my thoughts scrambled. My mind's eye could not see but my mind heard me chanting, "Never look back, never look back. Only forward, only forward." It's my own little aphorism, my mantra, to keep my mind whirring.

Seneca was at my apartment that night after my class, when I lurched into the bathroom and threw up in the sink, tossing my head back and looking in the mirror as I brushed my teeth. Seneca quoted again: *For the only safe harbour in this life's tossing, troubled sea is to refuse to be bothered about what the future will bring and to stand ready and confident* . . . Some unknown part of myself looking for help in outlandish places. *Every hour of the day countless situations arise that call for advice, and for that advice we have to look to philosophy.*

They were supposed to be Letters to Lucilius but they had become Letters to Seraphina.

Off I hurtled, for the first time. No more classes, no more paperweights reminding me of what I did, what my mother asked me to do.

The exhilaration of running from yourself, of fleeing your thoughts, your guilt, the sweet momentum you gain when imagination sends a phantom philosopher in pursuit. Never look back, only forward.

BIRDIE WHIPS AROUND ANOTHER corner and I start to fly but now my bra is caught on a hook on the van wall and so I snap back and dangle there, arms flapping. Clarity is my enemy, the inflictor of pain. What comes before or after doesn't matter. My own life spiralling me into vertigo, mixing it all up. *My haggard mother driving me to the antique shop in Seabury. To slimy Mr. Burgess. Do whatever he asks. He'll give us the best price. My mother's eyes red from lack of sleep, sorting through the mass of bills and collection notices.*

The reality is, I hang here like a disabled bat in a red bra. I wore a red bra under my wedding dress because it seemed the only vestige of the rogue I had thought I was. Until we were in front of the preacher.

Actually it started when I saw Elizabeth's head, the back of her head. I admired her hair and thought what a nice style it was, wondered why it was done so daintily, with little violets in it. She didn't normally dress like that. The perfection of her bridesmaid updo made my eyes water. But the flowers became fuzzy, one big blob of purple. The floor seemed to tilt. I wondered about this too until I heard, *"Psssst."* I jumped. But it was a female voice, not the Roman. It was Birdie. She was at the back, by the door. "Get going. It's time."

The violets were blurry because they were now up front at the altar with Darren and the preacher and Darren's best friend from university who makes bad jokes and smacks everyone on the shoulder. I was still standing at the back of the church. And it all hazed over. The room was tipping. I put my arms out for balance but still the hardwood floor seemed to slant, an illusion.

"Go." At least Birdie's voice was clear. And so I went. I went up to the front through the fuzziness, and I wondered if they could see my red bra, at least the suggestion of the bra. It was lacy, really pretty — a push-up. But I didn't think so. I was the only one who knew about it besides Elizabeth, who had helped me dress. The antique dealer sat in a pew, winking, his wife beside him smiling, wiping a tear with a lace hanky. He was wearing a black suit and sunglasses, like an undercover agent sent from my past, lest I forget my snafus, my terrible choices. *Our little secret, Serrie. Come again and I'll give you a good price on what you bring next, as long as you can stay and visit.*

My mother invited him to the wedding. *Bucolic Valley. Claustrophobic country life along those sickly-sweet country roads. Keeping up appearances.*

I looked away from the Burgesses. I focused on the teeth. There were so many teeth. Probably because people were smiling. At weddings people usually smile, right? Goddamn, it was like being surrounded by Mormons. I always think of Mormons as people with big white teeth. But no one was Mormon here. It was the Foster First United Church. My face was rigid with an enormous pink lipsticked smile. Inside I was panicking, electric zaps in my brain, my heart thrashing against my ribs. What if Seneca appeared, chastising me, imploring me to stand fast and quiet, come to terms with my past?

The teeth became like a haze of cotton and the music was squeaking and droning. God, it was terrible, which surprised me — my brother is a concert violinist. I must have put my hands to my ears because Elizabeth asked me if I was okay. I could see her then, her brown eyes, and I could see her lips moving but I only heard the *okay?* part. She knew I was going to bail and I knew I was going to bail and Birdie must have been suspecting it back there by the doors where she had been coordinating it all, and I shook my head at Elizabeth and my eyes filled up with tears because even I'm not so selfish I didn't feel a bit of guilt.

I bolted. I was carried away on wings woven with fine threads of thrill and speed, Seneca behind me shouting *a plant which is frequently moved never grows strong*. Shut up, Seneca, I shouted back at the fat, miniature floating man only I could see.

Tits to the wind. The second vamoose. The last bailout. I ran down the aisle and Elizabeth ran after me, the pews filled with tall, gasping shadows. At the steps, I threw the flowers away and ripped off the bodice of the dress. Birdie was saying, "What the fuck are you doing, Seraphina?" and I was saying, "Get your van, get your van."

And she did. She went and got the van and I was running down the street to the corner with Elizabeth behind me and I would have kept running if Birdie hadn't roared up.

"Serrie, get in. Get in the fucking van. How could you do this?"

And now I am dangling here, dying for a smoke. "Can someone give me a cigarette?" Birdie rummages through her purse, one hand on the wheel, one hand passing back a cigarette which Elizabeth sticks in my mouth and lights. They don't notice I'm hooked to the wall. They must know. They do know. This is where they want me.

The stillness of this tiny suspended moment is excruciating. Antique dealer wants to crawl into my head. *Such bad breath. So heavy. Now run home to your mother. Sticky crotch. Old-man sweat on my soft teenage skin. Washing up in the bathroom. Crying on the walk home, money in my pocket.*

As soon as I got in the van on the church corner, I used Birdie's phone — my first time using a cellphone — to book a ticket. "I want to go to Europe, anywhere in Europe," I told the airline guy. "Halifax to Europe. Right now. Right now." I gave Elizabeth's credit card number. She was crying. She took the phone from me and called her cousin Cindy and told her to go to my mother's house at the top of the Mountain on the Lupin Cove Road. She should pack me a bag, the old black hat-box suitcase. We would meet her at my house as soon as we could.

"The key is in the outhouse out back. Just get there as fast as you can and pack. Put anything in the suit-case," Elizabeth yells into the phone. "Some shorts, a bathing suit. Just go through Serrie's drawers." She turns red as she listens. "Don't ask questions. Just pack it," she screams, "and don't ask me why. And don't call me Bethie. My name is Elizabeth."

We don't talk while Birdie drives us all the way over the Valley floor and up the Mountain to my rundown house. Elizabeth will deal with my mother after I'm gone. She'll tell her I wasn't ready for marriage. Elizabeth understands wanting to leave the past behind. I won't speak to my mother for months. Elizabeth suspects. She remembers high school. She knows I can't stay in the Valley. Best-friend intuition. And then there is Seneca. Go away, Seneca, I whisper, but he holds up his hand and speaks: *A change of character, not a change of air, is what you need. Though you cross the countless ocean; though, to use the words of our poet Virgil, "Lands and towns are left astern," whatever your destination, you will be followed by your failings.*

The van hits a bump. I close my eyes and when I open them, Seneca is gone.

Cindy is standing on the rotting verandah with the old hat-box suitcase when we get to my house. We screech to a stop. Elizabeth slides the van door open. Cindy's eyes pop wide open when she sees me dangling there. I laugh. Her shock delights me. She opens her mouth but says nothing as Elizabeth leans out and grabs the case, sliding the door shut as she leans back in.

"How about another smoke?" I ask once we're roaring on the highway to the airport.

"How about shutting up, Serrie? Who is Seneca?" Elizabeth's face is still red.

Birdie stomps the brakes. "Let it go, Elizabeth."

I snap like undies on a clothesline. Elizabeth jerks forward.

Birdie floors it now and yells over her shoulder, "Shut up, Elizabeth. It's over now. Just shut up. Seneca is probably just some idiot Serrie met in a bar." She hands another lighter back to Elizabeth who lights me another cigarette and sticks it in my mouth. She leaves me hanging there in the bra and digs through the black case, looking for something for me to wear.

"Fuck, don't burn me."

Elizabeth is trying to pull a tattered white T-shirt over my head, but I'm still hooked. She's dressing me like I'm a baby, a big, smoking baby. We hit another corner and I fall off the van wall, landing on top of Elizabeth, who crashes over and lies there, crying. I stub the cigarette out on the metal floor, sit up, and put my arms through the sleeves. It is my superhero costume. The queen of the bolt. I close my eyes and can hear the Stoic say, *Devotion to what is right is simple, devotion to what is wrong is complex and admits infinite variations.*

I turn around at Security. They're standing there, Elizabeth and Birdie, in Tyrian purple bridesmaid dresses, arms around each other, Seneca floating at the left. *But the chief cause of this disease, in my opinion, is an attitude of disdain for a normal existence.* They don't move, and I can't stand that. Birdie's crying now too. "Tits to the wind, Serrie. Tits to the wind."

And I turn my back on the floating Stoic and the Bail-out Squad.

I SEE THE OCEAN from the airplane window. In my mind there is a whisper... *Beyond all things is the sea, Seraphina.* Before Seneca can materialize, the man beside me coughs and pokes his elbow into my ribs. He wants to talk about jet lag. I don't want to talk about jet lag. I want a gin and tonic. I want five gin and tonics. Anything to bring back the blur. I have twelve hours of travel ahead and I want to spend it in a haze, with fuzzy voices and muted sounds lulling me into sleep so time will blink by. So the imagined philosopher won't appear. I want to forget everything I've ever learned. I want oblivion right now. But the man beside me wants to talk about the "New Canadians" (he means Asians). In his trimmed beard, nice shirt, clean glasses, casual shoes, I-have-a-nice-home-in-the-suburbs-with-a-few-kids-and-a-wife way, he wants to talk about "the invasion."

"I haven't been to Vancouver," I say.

"Aren't you going to Vancouver?" he wants to know.

"I get off in Toronto, and then I'm heading for Zurich." I yawn although I want to scream.

He loves chocolate and the Alps.

I love the Walkman Cindy packed and I reach to put it on. There is one really old cassette, John Denver, singing "Sweet Surrender."

The man keeps talking. I smile and touch my headphones. He keeps talking. Fuck. I mean what's with some people? I say, "I can't hear you."

He says I should lower the volume.

I tell him it's stuck at ten and lie back and shut my eyes. I'm not the kind of girl to cry to country music. I prefer a lyre. He pokes me in the side and asks if I want dinner. I want him to shut up. I wonder if he will have a brain aneurism. I say I'm sick. The dial moves and the loud music distorts into perfection but I know he is still talking. At least the Stoic has abandoned me.

Later I see the airplane man at a payphone when I'm looking for the next gate. I walk by with the Walkman attached, but it isn't on.

He winks. Looks at my tits. "Nice bra, baby."

I squint and he fades into the crowd that surges forward, these faceless people arriving and departing and arriving and departing. Then I run to the gate, those tits of mine gone to the wind once more. Never look back, I hum to myself, only forward, only forward. There before me, hovering, as usual, a bit to the left, is the thing in the toga. *Every day, every hour sees a change in you, although the ravages of time are easier to see in others; in your own case they are far less obvious.*

THE BLUE SKY ABOVE the Atlantic reminds me of Darren's eyes. At least they were bright and clear. *For those who follow nature everything is easy and straightforward, whereas for those who fight against her life is just like rowing against the stream.* I close my eyes and wait for sleep to come and it does, leaving when the plane is on approach, when I see Lake Zurich from the airplane window, the Alps, the white peaks soaring into endless blue, the future wide open. We touch down in Switzerland. I cruise through Customs, holding up my passport and giggling because suddenly it seems so funny I'm here and it's suppertime in Nova Scotia and bedtime in Zurich.

THE FLYING
SQUIRREL SERMON

I have seen them riding seaward on the waves
Combing the white hair of the waves blown back
When the wind blows the water white and black.
We have lingered in the chambers of the sea

By sea-girls wreathed with seaweed red and brown
Till human voices wake us, and we drown.
— T.S. Eliot, "The Love Song of J. Alfred Prufrock"

ONDINE PARKED HER CAR in the dusty driveway. It was hotter than she had imagined it would be this close to the water, but the house was on a dirt road up from the bay, so sea breezes were probably intermittent. The still air was humid and dense, as though it were a massive resting creature pressing in upon her, a presence she had to push through even as it enveloped her.

It had seemed like a good idea to come out and do the research in person. In fact, it was the only way. The old woman hadn't answered any of the letters Ondine had sent. And she had no phone. It was almost unheard of, someone without a phone, let alone internet. It was no surprise Ondine's cellphone didn't work here. Halfway up the mountain she noticed she had no signal when she checked her texts, something she knew better than to do while she was driving but did anyway because there wasn't a single other car on the road.

She had a feeling of solitude, which then gave her a sense a safety. She knew it was false. All it would take was one deer leaping out from the trees, or a child appearing at the side of the road on a bicycle, something unexpected... and then life irrevocably changed. It was hard to believe, with the blue sky, the fields of hay and wildflowers, that there could be any danger here. But this was the place of her family legends, of women evanescing, of dangerous forest streams and sudden fogs.

Ondine had taken a chance and booked a flight, rented a car, and then undertook the five-hour drive through the country and up and over the mountain, finally to this dirt road. She didn't have an actual civic address. Her grandmother had told her there was only one house on the Flying Squirrel Road, about fifty miles from a place called Lupin Cove. Ondine planned to interview anyone she could find, if she could actually locate the house, and then drive back and stay at the airport hotel. But even Google Maps didn't show anything when she did a search for the road name.

Her grandmother had retreated more and more from reality and it was difficult to know whether what she'd whispered was truth or fantasy, or if the stories were a weave of both. That was often the case, Ondine had discovered in her research. Her grandmother had longed for the seashore and sometimes hadn't recognized the people around her. She was cryptic and lapsed into long silences. Ondine regretted not doing more formal interviews with her grandmother while she could—before, that is, she walked out of the country nursing home when the door to her unit had been propped open by a new nurse. They never found her body. The police didn't make much of an effort to find someone that elderly. They figured she had fallen into a ravine or been eaten by coyotes, although they had put it more delicately.

Ondine saw the old woman sitting on the porch as soon as she pulled into the driveway. Her frizzy silver hair flowed around her shoulders and deep wrinkles rippled through her face. Ondine had expected someone much younger, but realized that of course her grandmother had spoken as though still a teenager, her mind floating through all the years of her life and anchoring in her girlhood. Ondine was nervous. She sat in the car with her hands on the steering wheel, surprised by her own inability to bring professional objectivity to her personal life.

As soon as the car engine was off, a seagull squawked and the old woman called out to Ondine. "Young woman, are you lost or is this your destination?" She didn't seem surprised to see her. It was Ondine who was surprised the place even existed, how it wasn't a fictional setting in a story passed down within her family.

Ondine got out of the car but the woman didn't get up or beckon her to the house. Ondine was not sure what to do. She gave what she hoped was a friendly wave. "I think this is the right place. My grandmother said she grew up on the Flying Squirrel Road. I always promised her I would come back to visit when she died." Ondine didn't begin explaining the complicated story of her grandmother's end.

"Well, imagine! Isn't that nice of you to respect her wishes. No doubt she'll be pleased. It's some hot today. What a summer. It'll be cooler down by the water. Cool and foggy but it will be most welcome. It's been a long time in coming. I wasn't sure who could be pulling into my driveway. My friends are all passed away now and there are only a few distant cousins but I don't want a thing to do with their corruption."

The old woman cleared her throat as Ondine introduced herself and explained she was here to do some research for her dissertation on oral tradition as a method of cultural preservation. The old lady didn't say a word but she began laughing until she started coughing and hacking, each heave of her chest seeming to be the last. It subsided and she sat there in her chair in the dense afternoon heat. "Come on up and have a rest. You've got that parched look to you which comes from living inland."

Ondine walked over the overgrown path to the front verandah. There was a small pond in front of the house with an old fountain in the centre, nothing coming out of the odd, fishlike sculpture in the middle. She looked up from the fountain to see the old woman watching her carefully. She didn't even seem to blink. Ondine couldn't interpret much from the old woman's face, which was like a piece of crumpled linen. She was fanning herself with an antique hand-held fan. She held a cane in the other and with it she summoned Ondine up the rotting steps and gestured toward an old bench.

Ondine sat down and took out her phone and a small black notebook and pen. "Perhaps you could just tell me some of your childhood stories, events of your life. Is it okay if I record you?" She showed the woman her phone and explained it worked as a recording device as well.

"Be my guest." The old woman snorted as though it was amusing, as though technology wasn't something to be taken seriously. "But we must get started for we won't have long," she said.

"Well, I'm doing research on a specific story, a legend, which originates from this area, of women who disappeared. It's for my Ph.D. in cultural anthropology, on storytelling."

Ondine knew most of these women were related to her but did not mention she had heard about this from her grandmother. That part was personal. She didn't want the old lady to know anything personal about her. How she wasn't actually doing a dissertation—it was already completed. She had graduated. It was the bedtime stories her grandmother had told her as a child, and then her final ramblings, which had led Ondine back to this godforsaken place on the dusty dirt road.

The old woman shrugged, like none of this was news to her, like she had been expecting Ondine's visit for a long time. She immediately began talking. "Ondine was my sister's middle name, my sister Rose Ondine. It's so old-fashioned, such a pretty name. An old family name."

She'd gone there right away, Ondine noticed. *Her sister.* Before Ondine could make too much of it, the old woman raised her hand and pointed out toward the ocean, which Ondine could barely see through the trees.

"We don't have much time on account of the tides. The tide's coming in, you see. The weather might turn. I expect you'll appreciate that like we all do."

It was so humid Ondine's cotton sundress was soaked in sweat even though she was sitting still. "Yes, though a cool breeze would be nice."

The old woman handed Ondine her wooden folding fan. It was painted black, with iridescent abalone shell inlaid in the handle and along the slats. It was a relief to sit and listen. That was just as well, since the old lady did not seem the sort who would take kindly to interruptions or questions. "This belonged to my sister, and to my mother before her. It's just like us women, it's far tougher than it looks, so don't be shy, give it a good flutter. Yes, that's right. Isn't it a joyous thing when the air has some movement? Now, young Ondine, let me tell you I don't know exactly where my sister went, although I've always had my ideas. It's time I finally spoke to this. We come from a family of preachers and they say the gift of oration runs in our blood. But I never wanted to be no preacher. That comes from my daddy's side. Other things run in our blood from my mother's side, or at least, so they say. But if I'm called to I will tell our story. I'm near the end of my time now. The signs have come."

The old lady kept looking at her, so Ondine nodded as though she understood. But she didn't. She looked out from the verandah—at the front of the house, near the small pond with the dried-up fountain, there was a flower garden covered in brown and red seaweed with a few small white roses poking through.

"There's been many over the years who've vanished or come to unfortunate ends. Our mother was the first to vanish, leaving me and Rose and our brother, Hiram, alone with our father. Little Hiram was only three years old. I myself was only five, so it's hard to recall exactly what happened to our mother. But Rose was seven years old and she remembered, even though she would not speak of it to us, not even when we were a bit older and started asking her about where our mother had got to.

"Our daddy called himself a preacher but he was nothing more than the tyrant of the Flying Squirrel Road. I did not grieve him when he died.

"The next to disappear was my sister, Rose, when she was just a teenager, nine years after our mother. And then there were the terrible deaths. First, a boy named Elmore, only fourteen years old. And many years later, when I was a grown woman with my own baby, Elmore's mother was murdered. Elmore's mother had become my stepmother after her husband was found dead on the beach. Her death was especially hard on me, although my father didn't seem moved by her demise any more than he was by our mother's disappearance. Both Elmore and my stepmother left this earth in gruesome fashion. Finally, my daddy came to his long-suffering end, followed not long after by my little brother, Hiram. And there was my little girl who died. And then my own malicious husband."

Ondine was shocked by the list of dead and missing. It was more people than she had realized. She had some of these names written in her notes but hearing the old woman rhyme off the names so quickly was disturbing. The way she told the story, it was as though this had happened recently. Her memory was remarkable, unless she was half senile and making it up. The old woman stopped talking and the air was very still without her voice ringing out. She had a small scowl on her face as she stared at Ondine.

For a second it seemed the old woman had been listening to her thoughts, that she was annoyed Ondine would doubt her mental acuity. Ondine's shock must have shown on her face. She was annoyed with herself for being unable to maintain professional composure.

But the old woman's face softened and she pointed at Ondine. "Keep fanning yourself, my dear, or you might faint. I'll take you for a walk down to the beach later but you'll have to get your strength up."

The fan was in Ondine's lap. She hadn't realized she had set it there, so lost had she been in the old woman's astonishing story.

"I was only fourteen when Rose went away, and I've missed her every day right up until this moment. And when I was grown, it was my stepmother's end which wounded me deep, because I was a young mother then myself. You realize then how little you can do to protect even the most vulnerable.

"I can tell you they don't know where my stepmother's head's buried. It ain't with her body. It went in the graveyard, along with one of her arms and her two legs, chopped off like they was pieces of firewood, can you believe it? Don't look so shocked, girl! We were poor. And of course they didn't want any gawkers coming round. The pieces of her were laid down in the earth. They didn't use no coffin, just wrapped my stepmother up in a soft, flowered cloth, the kind she made her dresses from, and then wrapped her parts around again with velvet. I know this for I was there when my stepmother's sisters gathered up the fabric.

"It was the end of summer and still hot, so they had to put her in the earth fast and quick. Exact same weather we have today, I'll have you know. Her sisters have all since departed this earth. Those were the old ways and sometimes those old ways stay behind when the time they arose from has passed. They held onto the old ways, those ladies, I'll tell you. And that's what they instructed, to hold on to the old ways, which I'm now telling you, young Ondine. They wrapped my stepmother up by the light of the moon. Not because they were superstitious but because they didn't want no attention.

"She was my stepmother but I loved her dearly. You understand . . . sometimes people leave us, even the wee ones." The old lady coughed and then got up with an unexpected agility for one so stooped and curved, as though for decades she had bent over tidal pools and leaned from a lobster boat hauling traps. She opened the screen door and disappeared down the hall. Ondine could hear clunking inside. She looked out over the road, the bay a soft blue, glistening under the broiling afternoon sun. The shade of the verandah was a sanctuary.

Ondine saw the door knocker fixed to the outside wall beside the door. It was old and small, made of tarnished brass, and resembled something out of the sea — with a curved head, fins, and a long tail. The wooden door handle was similar, a long, carved fish tail with countless detailed brass scales forming the handle. It looked almost like a sea horse, but Ondine couldn't be sure without a closer look.

The old lady came back out and Ondine was surprised how she hadn't heard her come down the hall, at how quiet she was, even with a cane. She took a sip of water out of a glass jar sitting on the railing. The old woman didn't offer Ondine anything to drink, but she carefully watched her as she took note of the knocker and handle, noting how Ondine's eyes moved slowly up and down the objects. Ondine figured she was used to people stopping by, lost, not able to use their phones to figure out where they were, gawking at the old, rundown house and all its strange features. There was intricate stained glass in the main door of the house but it was impossible to see the detail from where Ondine was sitting.

The old woman took a breath and continued speaking as she sat down. "There were those who thought my stepmother brought it on herself, and people like my husband who said my father was innocent. But in all our minds we kept thinking of my stepmother's son, Elmore, who'd died years before, when he fell from a truck. And of course, my sister, Rose, who disappeared. Rose Ondine. You look so much like Rose ... like I imagine she would have looked if I ever laid eyes on her when she was grown up.

"They said Rose was pregnant and took off in the night. I don't know if that's what happened. I do know the men around here were always worried how their women wouldn't do as they said. That was always a problem. They said it was a curse, a curse which got awakened when my stepmother got murdered. If she was taken care of, if you don't mind me putting it that way, then perhaps things would be normal around here, and women would do as their husbands said. But it only got worse after that. Violence never wastes its breath singing a lullaby."

Something screeched from the field across the road, and Ondine jumped. Maybe a cicada, she thought. The old lady looked at her. "Don't mind the creatures. There ain't nothing to be afraid of. Those men said my father didn't kill my mother or my stepmother, just like they said he didn't kill my sister. Of course there was no bodies when it come to my sister, Rose, and our mother. But there are some things they never knew about Rose. Or my stepmother. Things those women kept hid.

"And now here you are, wanting to know. 'Tell me your stories,' you say.

"My stepmother had such a pretty amethyst ring her first husband gave her and she wore it on her right ring finger, a sparkling amethyst ring he picked up off the beach, as though it had been left there for him to discover. It was so long ago but it looked like the one upon your finger, young Ondine. It was a tradition in these parts for some women to have purple gemstones gathered from the shore, you know. Did your grandmother tell you that?"

Ondine touched the ring on her sweaty finger without looking down, her eyes fixed on the old lady's impenetrable face.

"They say my stepmother's first husband drowned in the bay, his face buried in a mound of seaweed when the tide washed his body in on the shore. It was common knowledge he was unfaithful, breaking her heart. They said he had gone out for a midnight rendezvous with some girl who lived down in the Valley. After he was buried, my stepmother was left alone on the big old farm and my daddy desired it. It had been a lot of years since our mother and Rose disappeared, and he finally wanted to get away from our place here and the sounds and voices he heard in the woods at night, sounds right inside this house.

"Daddy had no interest in our stepmother's grey

hair or the lines on her face, but he said the words he thought would charm her. They did, but not enough for her to put the land title in his name and that sent Daddy into a cold quiet rage. My stepmother wore his thin gold band on her ring finger, but even when they had their little marriage with the justice of the peace, she kept wearing that amethyst from her first husband on her other hand. My stepmother carried a bouquet of small white buds she'd cut from a rose bush my sister planted when she was young."

Ondine wasn't going to tell the old woman that the ring Ondine was wearing had been given to her by her grandmother, who had also told her it was a family heirloom she had inherited. But the old woman already seemed to know this. Ondine had no idea how it would have found its way to her grandmother. If the old woman knew, she wasn't letting on.

"No one ever could discern what became of the ring, so it must have been still on her hand, the one that went missing along with her head. It made my daddy so angry she wouldn't take it off, but they was both middle-aged when they got married and my stepmother said you couldn't put the past behind you like that.

"Well, my father thought he was someone who could put anything behind him but he could not get away from what he was hearing in the yard and the farmhouse at night."

She looked at Ondine and shrugged her shoulder toward the house and then pointed, in case Ondine was confused. "This house."

THE OLD LADY SQUEEZED her eyes shut, as though she'd just realized she had somewhere to be soon. A large bird landed on the weathered verandah railing. Ondine didn't know what kind of bird it was, a sea bird of some sort. It perched there while the woman kept talking, as though it was waiting for her to pause. It was disturbing. The old woman's voice was very loud now and she kept raising her hand. It was unnerving, although the bird didn't seem to mind. Ondine felt impatient and considered interrupting to say she had to leave, that she had miscalculated her time. But now she was worried that if she interrupted the old lady she would be infuriated, or might have some sort of attack.

"Yes, *Don't come around no more* is what my father told them, whenever they sent any of them do-goodies up here on the Lonely Road, up and over the Mountain and then halfways across before turning down the dirt road to our farm. Spies is what he called them all, the social workers, the police, even the preachers. Daddy said they should have been going after the whore who ran off, leaving Rose in charge of me and Hiram. That was what he called our mother. Wasn't that a nice way to talk to your children? He was a mean old thing. I never talked so to my little girl.

"Rose was two years older than me and she was just a child herself but she seemed like a grown up, standing in front of us when our father would have a temper, shaking her finger at him. Everybody loved Rose, even our daddy. He was afraid of Rose, though. 'Those sea-green eyes are full of secrets,' he'd yell when she'd stand there admonishing him. 'You've got salt water in your veins, but you're a good girl, Rosie. I know you are. You wouldn't do nothing bad to your father.'"

The woman opened her eyes then, and looked at Ondine and shook her finger. "You might see an old woman but inside, behind these eyes, I ain't no old woman. That's what you young people don't understand. I know because I was young too once. Nothing ain't ever clear until the end. Until it's too late. My grandfather was a preacher and he said everything you do takes you to the place where you learn a lesson. When you learn the lesson then you can look back and see what all you went through was about. Ain't no sense in moaning about what's happening or why. You just got to survive it. And testify."

She stood up and grabbed her cane, which had been leaning on the chair. She thumped the cane three times as though she were sending a signal. The bird flew away, letting out a few squawks as it lifted off the railing. "You better be careful what you ask me or I'll be telling you what my daddy said, that you better not come around here no more, with your recorders and your notebooks. You're lucky I'm not like Daddy. That's what he would say and just like I said it now, hissing like a snake, curling the right side of his lip up when he said *Missy*. 'Missy' is a nice word but not how he said it. He could even make the names of flowers sound like horrible swear words and curses—violet, lilac, honeysuckle, peach blossom. He made all them words reek like shit.

"I can tell from your face you think this is just foolish talk from an old lady. The eyes don't lie. It is understandable you would think my talk foolish. You remind me of someone, but right now I can't recall who. Give me a bit of time. It will come to me."

In the terrible heat, Ondine shivered. But it was occurring to her that the old woman *already knew* who she was and understood why Ondine was here. She was just not ready to share that yet.

THE OLD WOMAN HAD gone back in the house and Ondine listened to her walking down the hall, muttering to herself. Ondine got up to timidly open the screen door and follow her inside and noticed then that the stained glass was very old—shades of blue and grey, waves with small translucent shapes in the midst of them, an opalescent sky overhead the heaving green glass sea. "Pretty, isn't it?" Ondine jumped. She hadn't heard her come back. The woman spoke to Ondine through the dark screen. "Antique dealers always want to buy the door right off the house. They might do so one day when I am gone but they'd do well to keep that door from ever attaching to any other house. My daddy was terrified of it."

She came outside, handed Ondine a glass of what looked like iced tea and sat down again. "Have a sip of that tonic. It will restore you. What do I think happened to Rose, you want to know? Ain't no one asked me that in a long time. Such a long time. Everyone always said she was delicate like the tiny plovers which run along the sand at low tide. Living up here on the Mountain, things don't seem to change much. They won't ever pave these roads, and with the mists and fogs blowing through all them gullies and hollers and ravines, they can't get their satellites to work, or them gadgets and phones they love so. That's just as well."

The old lady was watching Ondine holding the glass, waiting for her to sip. Ondine set the fan down on the verandah railing and looked at the murky liquid. It was a rusty red with an unusual smell, but Ondine was thirsty and her thirst overcame her aversion. She took a small taste. It was tangy and sweet, and she gulped the cold drink down and wiped her lips while the woman resumed talking.

"Some places don't want to change. It looks just the same here as it always did. Rose could stroll under those old trees just like all them years ago, calling over to the horses in the summer pasture, flower petals falling at her feet. She planted that big sugar maple there. You can see the horses by the tree. A horse loves some shade. They ain't the same horses but they're related. Everyone up here is. The horses loved Rose. It's one of the reasons my father was always respectful to her. The draught horses wouldn't tolerate him being cruel to a woman. And they was great big ones, shire horses.

"For years I would sit here on the verandah looking down the road over there and then to the meadow across from the house, right across the way, expecting Rose to appear by the fountain. You'd hear her first. She'd sing when she'd go walking. Said it kept the coyotes away and celebrated Holy Mother Mercy all at the same time. It didn't protect her enough, in the end, because Rose never walked back down that road again. But I don't think it was animals that got her. I think she got away."

Ondine was still sweating and a little draft lifted up and over the verandah railing, caressing her face. She felt dizzy and wondered if she needed more to drink or if the cold infusion itself had made her feel so disoriented.

"I see you aren't making any notes. And your recording device has shut off."

Ondine looked down. Her notebook and her phone were in her lap. The battery had died. She was stunned. She was sure she'd charged it. Her technical skills from years of research had been so reliable, habitual. The battery should have lasted for hours.

"See the whitecaps on the bay? The wind has come up. The tide is coming in now, as I said earlier it would do. I don't suppose you've ever been to the island out there? Those cliffs make it look like a fortress. Parker Island is the true name but most people just call it the Island. It's a curious landscape here, ain't it? Deep forest to the south behind the house, but here by the front verandah the land slopes downward for a few miles through the fields until it drops right off to the beach by the bay you're looking at. I suppose if my great-grandfather never cleared them fields you'd think we were landlocked. But I always said being landlocked ain't nothing but a state of mind. Closer to the shore there's a constant wind but set back up here away from the water it's only occasional. It comes when it sees fit. Rose loved the smell—pine and moss from the forest, and woven through with salt water. I take the sea air for medicinal purposes, for my lungs.

No doubt you'll notice when you leave this road you'll feel light-headed."

Ondine already felt light-headed. "Well, I should be leaving soon. It's a long drive back to the airport and my phone has died. And I've taken up enough of your time."

The old woman gazed at Ondine. "Time is all I've had these long years, time and all these stories." She leaned back in her chair and closed her eyes briefly and then opened them. Ondine handed the old woman the fan, wondering if she too was feeling woozy.

The old woman took the fan in her crooked fingers and placed it beside her leg on the seat of the chair. She let out a long sigh.

"I suppose you want an answer before you go. Answering your questions involves going back years and years. Rose disappeared after Elmore died on the farm. Elmore was my stepmother's son, from her first marriage. He was a slow boy who would come and work. Rose was always so kind to him and our brother, Hiram, was so jealous. He was just like our daddy by the time he was becoming a man. Hiram couldn't stand Rose paying attention to anyone but him. He even got mad if she spent time helping me. Poor Elmore was going to some fancy church camp that summer, down in the Valley on Lake of Redemption. Some missy hissy got him some money from a fund for country children. He was a sweet boy. Quiet in his mind but real kind.

Elmore never made it to the camp. He was only four-teen. What a pity it was. Hiram said it was my fault, that I was driving too fast down the Flying Squirrel Road, but it was a lie.

"Hiram was in the passenger seat of the truck when we was driving out back to the strawberry fields. He was two years younger than me and four years younger than Rose. She was just turned sixteen that summer. Rose almost run the whole farm by herself. Hiram was mad he couldn't be the man in charge but had to sit with his sister at the wheel. Hiram dared not say one word to Daddy for fear of the horse whip on his back. He surely did go on to Rose about how it weren't fair. He'd never take a turn in the back or stand alongside the passenger side of the cab on them running boards. That's where Hiram made the dirt-poor kids stand who came to work on the farm. July is always such a hot month and you'd kill for a ride even just twenty feet.

"They held onto the truck with one hand and their hats with the other so the wind wouldn't steal them away into the woods. "I remember how Elmore was standing on the running board outside the passenger door, the window rolled down, and Hiram talking his bullshit about how he was this expert farmer, like he was lord of the strawberries. Strawberry pickers all over the truck. Elmore was there one minute, duck-ing from Hiram who was teasing him, and then he was gone. Hiram said the truck bounced and Elmore lost his footing. Hiram swore he was reaching his arm out the window to steady Elmore, not pulling his arm back in from pushing him.

"Daddy took the whip to Hiram until Rose came home from visiting Elmore's grieving mother. Hiram's back was bleeding. Rose got out the gun and held it at Daddy 'til he saw her and then he dropped the whip. He was afraid of her after that. And our brother Hiram was afraid of what Daddy would do to Rose. All spring Hiram said Daddy was planning something terrible. He was worrying Rose would spread lies about him.

"And sure enough, come the summer, a year after Elmore fell and hit his young head on the hard dirt, Rose vanished. It was the end of August, as it is now. We looked all over them roads and through the fields and forests and down on the beach. But no sir, we didn't find her, only her shoe and her straw hat in the woods by the stream. People said it all started with Elmore's death, how it all went bad after that. But it went bad long before."

THE SUN HAD COME around in the sky. It was late in the afternoon.

The old woman was impervious to the heat. She was like an animal, perfectly acclimatized to her environment. Part of Ondine wanted to leave, but a bigger part of her couldn't stop listening.

"Sometimes people leave and you never have no answers. That's what my father said, after the police stopped coming around a year after Rose went missing. At first he raged how someone killed her. Next he raged she took off like her filthy whore of a mother. We did not talk of Rose after that first year. Daddy would not allow no more speculation or discussion. He went quiet like something was coming for him. He got stranger in his mind. He heard things calling in the dark. Keep away the night birds, he'd yell. Don't go near the stream running down through the woods. Don't answer if anything comes knocking at the door. Close it tight and bolt it. Put down the windows and put rags around the crack at the bottom of the door. Don't let the mist seep in."

DARK CLOUDS WERE SLOWLY moving in from the northwest, above the lowering sun. Ondine wondered if there would be a lightning storm and the air would clear. She looked at her phone again. Useless thing. She set it on the railing.

The old lady's eyes were closed once more, lost in her story. "After Rose vanished just like our mother did, people whispered. I only know the bits I overheard, for no one would ever tell me the exact circumstances surrounding our mother's disappearance. But it was common knowledge she was tired of our father's constant fists and demands on her body.

"It wasn't so easy for us, of course, left behind on the Mountain with our father. He wouldn't let us speak of her. It may interest you to know our mother's name was also Ondine, like yours, like Rose's middle name. Our father insisted our mother was a loose woman who didn't care about her children. His story for the neighbours was she had taken off with a travelling salesman who had come along selling farm equipment. I have a memory of him wiping down the kitchen counter and floor early one morning. He'd never done a bit of cleaning before. There had been a loud noise. I came down the stairs crying. Rose came after me and put me to bed. But when we were older she would never discuss it with me, no matter how much I begged. She only said to be patient.

"Our father never changed. We saw this with our stepmother, who come along so many years later when Daddy decided he wanted a new wife.

"I still make my way down to my stepmother's grave and throw a few flowers about and say a prayer to Holy Mother Mercy. I would take you there, my dear, but we're almost out of time. The tide will be high. There was never any grave for my sister or my mother. Every

year in May I take spring ephemerals from the wood-
lands and throw them into the bay, hoping the waves
will carry the flowers to them. And at summer's end I
always pluck the petals from the last of the beach roses
and toss them into the sea."

Ondine saw then that the brass door knocker was
not a fish, but a woman with a tail. A mermaid. The
old woman watched her. "There's some things I won't
discuss, and I don't care if you need it for your history
projects and the like. I don't care who you are related
to. Ain't it pretty up here on the Mountain? People have
come by wanting to make an offer on that big old barn
off behind the house. They say they'll take it down
board by board and ship it far away and raise it up in
an alien land. And the work sheds as well. Imagine
that. Idiots, is what I say. And they call me crazy. You
couldn't pay me to set foot in a barn moved so many
miles. There'd be a curse on it.

"I love the Flying Squirrel Road, just sitting here.
Once upon a time the woods were full of flying squir-
rels and other beings that move through the night. The
house is close to the road but hardly any cars go by. I
used to worry about the distant relations who lived on
the Brow of Mountain Road overlooking the Valley,
that they'd come visiting. There was a wicked young
cousin who was a danger. I put a hex on this road to
keep her away. I'm just pulling your leg. They left a

number of years back and moved to Mercy Lake. If it's some tourist driving by, it just means they lost their way, but if I wave they seem to speed up. Maybe if I put some paint on the house. It peeled off years ago.

One guy who stopped come right up on the verandah when I was inside taking a shit. I could hear someone out there so I finished up my business and come out. Didn't he go off screaming. 'I thought this was an abandoned house,' he yelled as he went running off to his car. I sat in this here big rocker I'm in right now and watched the bastard tear off, dust flying off the dirt road. Then I looked down and saw I had left my gun out. I was just cleaning it. Always like to have it in working order, you know. It's not always loaded so don't you worry your pretty head.

"Some folks roam the world in search of wondrous sites, but living here there's no need. Wonder is all about. Sometimes when it's this hot I sit out on the verandah all day long and look out across that field to the blue bay. When I was little we still used horses for hay but then we got a few tractors. I still take a ride in the wagon sometimes. The old tractors are rusting in the fields. See them? Back there behind the barn. You're looking the wrong way. There's nothing in those old sheds and behind them — it ain't nothing but woods in the direction where you're looking. It's pretty in there, but you have to be careful what time you go in so you don't get short on light. No one wants to be in the woods when darkness falls.

"So look over at them fields. See the birch trees running alongside? And the line of poplars on the other? Listen to the wind chiming in those leaves. That old strawberry field is fallow now but it used to be one of the best strawberry fields we had. Sweet sun-warmed berries. The old tire swing still works. The tree branch up there went and grew all around the rusty chain it's hanging from. You can give it a try anytime you want. Sometimes when I'm up in my bed there's squeaky sounds. Don't go looking so scared. That's nothing more than the wind blowing.

"It's cool here on the verandah and under the tree where that dog is napping. Now the dog might look like he's sleeping under the sugar maple, the one I was telling you about which Rose planted, but if I snap my fingers he'll wake up and you won't be able to run. Don't worry though, I'm just kidding. He's an old dog. His bark is wicked mean but he's got the rheumatism and he is no longer able to run like he once did. You can't tell for how he's lying there in the shadows. Most of his teeth are gone. But you should never trust an old dog even if his teeth are gone. Sometimes they can turn.

"That dog, he don't like the heat. I don't mind it, for it never lasts long here, and when winter comes in, she don't let your thoughts linger on summer too long. She's that kind of lady. You love her and only her.

"You have to be careful telling stories. Some of them aren't yours to tell, you understand. Bad things happen when you steal them or change them. Did you know this?"

Ondine looked away, toward the small pond where something jumped. The fountain was running now. Maybe it had been the whole time and Ondine hadn't noticed.

"I CAME BACK UP here on the Mountain to the old place for good after I did my one and only time in jail. You didn't know that, now did you? Oh, I imagine I was almost forty by then. I can't remember. The whole decade just seems like it was one big long year. Daddy was gone finally, wizened up in a nursing home. I did go see him from time to time and he'd mutter away and say things that made me shudder. It was mostly nonsense. A bird flew in the window, he said, a bird with deep green eyes. A hand was crawling under his bed flashing a pretty ring with a purple stone. The mind does that for some. It collapses like the old barn over there will someday. But it never happened to me nor my brother. Our minds stayed sharp. Hiram's mind was still clear when he had the heart attack in the woods by the waterfall. I found him there when he was breathing out his last words, his regret over how Elmore died, how he always knew he'd pay for it.

"Some people, they get more astute when they get older. Hiram got craftier, but not one damn bit smarter or sensible, mind you. Always coming up with some way to get ahead that always involved putting someone else behind. Don't get me wrong. He'd do some nice things for you, if he wasn't trying to pull one over on you. He was the one who picked me up when I got out of jail. He testified to the judge about my character. Of course that don't mean much, for Hiram had no trouble lying for his kin. At least family loyalty ran in him. When my prison days were behind me I took over the family farm to work it in the old ways, with the horses, the plough.

"Look at old Lucretia Swindelle, they'd say, the lady farmer who did her husband in. They never found his body. I did not hide it. It wasn't me who took it.

"It was terrible sad when Rose went missing. I remember that morning. It was so hot and still. There was a horrible scream. Daddy said it was a peacock in the trees, one that came over from Petal's End from the idiot who had them as pets a long time ago.

"Let's go for a walk now, down to the water. You keep looking at the forest so I'll take you there. It's this time of day I like a walk, down by the stream, to the beach. The stream runs fast in the autumn, freezes in the winter, and then dries up in the early summer. But it's late August now so it will be flowing once more." The dog didn't move as they stood up and Ondine couldn't tell if it was dead or alive.

THEY WERE WALKING ALONG the path now, along the stream. Huge ferns grew on either side of the water, and the tree canopy made for such thick shade it felt like night never left the forest. The path was steep as it headed down through the woods to the beach and Ondine had to pay attention to every rock, every step. She was dizzy from the heat, from the exertion it was taking now to go down through the forest. There were occasional water pools, small waterfalls, and bits of red and brown seaweed scattered beside them.

The old woman's voice was high as she spoke quickly now, as though she was expecting something to happen and she might run out of time. "I can tell you to the best of my recollection, you understand, what happened to Rose. It's been some time and time is like the evening light. It softens and bends things as the eye falls upon them. Do you hear the crickets? Last week they come on in the early afternoon. Sometimes I feel like a cricket, something small and little, that no one can see, but still makes a noise. This is my summer song.

I sing it while I can now. There was a time I sang a song in every season...a song for autumn when the leaves went changing colours and the sky went deep blue. The air cold and crisp, smelling like rot...the smell of coming death. Then my winter song, the words I'd sing as I carried the wood in for my fire. The time of year when the blue would drain right out of the sky like something was sucking the colour out, a pale blue I would later see on my little girl's mouth when they pulled her from the river and her face was the colour of the winter clouds, and her lips was like petals dead upon the snow.

"When I look up at those black December skies with the big old moon rising up through the bare branches of the oak tree, I can hear Rose then, calling to the moon as she always did: *Over the mountain, over the sea, where my heart is longing to be, please let the light that shines on me, shine on the one I love.* But that was her December song and it stopped with her.

"You're looking the wrong way, back there by the woods. You turn your green eyes away from there, and look down over the bay. I know what you are.

"Look over the waves, my girl. They travelled by the stream, up to the land, looking for husbands and a soul. But woe betides the man who was charmed, for there was no forgiveness for any transgression against her or her children."

They had come out from the trees now to the rocky beach. There was a thick fog billowing in on the tide and the wind was cold and wet, the air briny. The old woman bent down and picked a few pink rose petals growing amidst the driftwood and shore brambles.

In the fog there seemed to be a high hum, as though there was a choir in the mists. There were dark shapes in the white haze as the waves crashed on the beach. The old woman threw her cane to the side and lifted up her arms. She raised her voice over the crash of the surf and looked at Ondine as she spoke. Her words were foreign and the exhortations were blown away by the wind as quickly as the old woman uttered them. And then the old lady was gone in the mists and the waves crashed in over Ondine's feet, and the spray felt like cold wet hands stroking her cheeks as she fell into the water, the pull of the turning tide taking her seaward.

ACKNOWLEDGEMENTS

I GRATEFULLY ACKNOWLEDGE THE Canada Council for the Arts, Arts Nova Scotia, and The Woodcock Fund/ Writers' Trust for funding which allowed me to write many of these stories. Thanks to the Atlantic Center for the Arts in New Smryna Beach, Florida, where I worked on several of these stories during a residency in 2005. Thanks to the Banff Centre for Arts and Creativity, where I finished these stories.

I acknowledge the privilege and honour in being a guest here in Mi'kma'ki, the unceded territory of the Mi'kmaq people for over 13,000 years.

Many thanks to Michelle MacAleese, my brilliant editor, for her instincts, openness, and generosity of spirit. Thanks to Janie Yoon for her unwavering faith in my work. Gratitude to the one-of-a-kind Sarah MacLachlan who one day appeared out of the Bay of Fundy fog on a dock in Parkers Cove and changed my life. To Melanie Little for meticulous and artful copyediting, and special thanks for her deep editorial touch on "Dead Time." Heartfelt thanks to the amazing team at House of Anansi Press for welcoming me and working so hard to collect these stories into a book and sending them into the world. Thank you to Joshua Greenspon for assistance with permissions. Thanks to Alysia Shewchuk for such a beautiful cover, managing editor Maria Golikova, proofreader Linda Pruessen, and Laura Meyer, publicist extraordinaire.

Many thanks to Kerry Lee Powell for spectacular notes on every single story. To Marianne Ward for her thoughtful comments on many of these stories. Love and gratitude to Marie Cameron for reading every draft. Thank you for reading earlier drafts of stories: Sandra Lambert, Belea Keeney, Cherie Dimaline, Liz Howard, Heather Morse, Kathryn Kuitenbrouwer, Adam Lewis Schroeder, Joceline Doucette, Rick Maddocks, Douglas Glover, Jessica Johnson, Dave Johnson, Dana Mills, and Greg Foran. Thanks to Joe Ollmann for discussion on comic arts, graphic design, drawing, and story narrative. Thank you to friend and colleague Amanda Peters of Glooscap First Nation for reading drafts, and for her enthusiasm for "Eyeball in Your Throat." Thanks to Madeleine Thien for reading numerous drafts of "The Diplomat" and "Late and Soon," and for such insightful notes. Thanks to Stephanie Domet who originally commissioned an earlier version of "Insomnis." Thank you to Silmy Abdullah and Shawk Alani for laughter in the mountains.

Thank you to Sue Goyette for quiet acts of kindness through many years. Thanks to Gwenyth Dwyn for all. Thanks to Lynn Coady and Rob Appleford for everything and especially acting out the various titles considered for the collection. Thank you to the band Nutsak. Thanks to Edible Art Café for the delicious food, to Jenny Osburn for mountain spirit and nutritional kindness. Thank you to my Women of Wolfville sisters: Wendy Eliott, Linda Wheeldon, Wendy LaPierre, Sandra Fyfe, Vida Mae Lantz, Sara Pound, and the powerful river of women in the wow community. Thanks to Box of Delights Bookshop, the Annapolis Valley Regional Library, and wonder librarian Angela Reynolds.

Thank you to, and in memoriam: Terri Luanna Mountain Borne Robinson da Silva (1974–2015), Helen Marie Veino Peill (1966–2016), Rhetta Dawn Morse (1969–2002), Jeannie Robinson (1948–2010), Sheila Diakiw (1933–2016), Murdy Daniel Conlin (my dad, 1930–2017), Teva Harrison (1976–2019).

Thanks to Mary Louise (my lovely mum), Orangie-Orange the literary cat, Patricia Acheson, Caroline Adderson, Nell den Heyer, Julia Baum, Dan Kehler, Millie LaPorte, Sara White, Robert and Jane

Woodworth, Rebecca Silver Slayter, Kim Kierans, Keith Maillard, Linda Svendsen, Peggy Thompson, Judge Chris Manning, Kent Hoffman, Mary Lynk, Noah Richler, Sara Selecky and her spectacular story course, Alexander MacLeod, Lisa Moore, Gary Craig Powell, Dr. Erika Dreifus, Genevieve Allen Hearn, Scott Campbell, Hardware Gallery, and Peter and Catherine Nathanson.

Some of these stories appeared in different forms in the following journals and anthologies: *Best Canadian Stories, Room Magazine, Fireweed, Numéro Cinq, The Coast, Victory Meat,* and *Review: Literature and Art of the Americas.* Earlier versions of "Occlusion" and "Desire Lines" were semi-finalists for the American Short Fiction Prize. A different form of "The Flying Squirrel Sermon" was long listed for the Commonwealth Short Story Prize. "Dead Time" was also published in a different form by Annick Press as part of a flip book shared with the multitalented Jen Sookfong Lee. A different form of "Beyond All Things Is the Sea" won the *blood + aphorisms* prize. A different version became the epilogue for my novel, *Heave.*

Thank you to Barbara Lipp and Armgard Lipp for language consultation. Thank you to Dr. Beverly Cassidy for research on depression, anxiety, memory, and sleep disorders, plus her overall medical brilliance. Thanks to Dr. Christopher Childs at the Sleep Disorders

Clinic in Halifax for insight on insomnia and the elusive quest for sleep. Thanks to Bria Stokesbury and Kate MacInnes-Adams at the Kings County Museum; Dan Conlin, historian at the National Museum of Immigration at Pier 21; Burlington community historians Pat Kemp and Anna Osburn of Burlington, North Mountain, Nova Scotia, for historical background about the horrific murder of Theresa Balsor McAuley Robinson 115 years ago. "The Flying Squirrel Sermon" is in her memory.

Research books consulted include: *Scenarios: Of Walking in Ice* by Werner Herzog; *Werner Herzog: A Guide for the Perplexed* (Conversations with Paul Cronin); *Every Night the Trees Disappear: Werner Herzog and the Making of Heart of Glass* by Alan Greenberg; *Scenarios* by Werner Herzog; *Letters from a Stoic, Epistulae Morales ad Lucilium* by Seneca, selected and translated by Robin Alexander Campbell; *Ad Lucilium espistulae morales* by Seneca; *Lusicus Annaeus, ca. 4 B.C. – 65 A.D.*, translated by Richard M. Gummere; *In Northern Mists: Arctic Exploration in Early Times* (Volume 1 of 2) by Fridtjof Nansen, translated by Arthur G. Chater, 1911; *Suasoriarum*, collected in *L. Annaei Senecae* (1557), Vol. 4, 620; *The Suasoriae of Seneca the Elder introductory essay, text, translation and explanatory notes; Being the 'Liber suasoriarum' of the work entitled L. Annaei Senecae Oratorum et rhetorum sententiae, divisiones, colores,* translated by W.A. Edward, 1928; *Sailing Alone Around the World* by Joshua Slocum, 1900; *The Strange Last Voyage of Donald Crowhurst* by Nicholas Tomalin and Ron Hall, 1970; *And the Sea Will Tell* by Vincent Bugliosi and Bruce Henderson; *Desire Lines, The shortest way from A to B* by Jan Dirk van der Berg; *Undine* by Friedrich Heinrich Karl de la Motte, Baron Fouqué; *Custom of the Country* by Edith Wharton; and the work of Paracelsus, German Swiss physician and alchemist, who was active during the German Renaissance.

With heartfelt appreciation to Dr. Sarah Emsley, always ready with an inspiring Jane Austen quotation for any occasion, for the marvellous literary friendship and correspondence about literature and the writing life, and for so carefully reading and commenting on the many drafts of these stories.

Thanks to my wonderful children, Silas, Angus, and Milo, whose joy and delight in daily adventures, be they travels abroad or twilight walks out back to see the beaver and night birds, endlessly inspire. And my darling husband, Andy Brown, whose magnificence has imprinted on my life as a watermark does on paper. Andy, my first reader and constant encourager—there are no words to express my appreciation for the miraculous life we have created together. Thank you for the graphic novels always there on the table by the woodstove, for the pink chair contemplations by the pond.

Finally, thanks to dear Maggie Estep, novelist and spoken word artist, who died unexpectedly in 2014. I had the privilege of working with Maggie in 2005 when she was a master artist at the Atlantic Center for the Arts in New Smyrna Beach, Florida. Maggie was instrumental in the shaping of "Late and Soon," supplying endless notes and encouragement even when I was back home in Nova Scotia. In 2015, I internet-stumbled upon a beautiful essay in *Vice* by writer Chloe Caldwell commemorating Maggie's final years in Hudson, New York. I've read "Maggie and Me: My Last Days with the Legendary Maggie Estep" countless times. My heart breaks every time I read it when Maggie briefly lives again. With Chloe's permission, I quote a line from the essay: "The owner of the yoga studio where Maggie taught said a few words, about how some people are suns and some people are moons, but then there was Maggie, who was a shooting star."

Whether we are suns or moons, shooting stars or waves that break upon the shore, may we all find some of that brightness which Maggie strew about wherever she went.

Thank you for reading these stories.

KATE INGLIS

CHRISTY ANN CONLIN is the author of two acclaimed novels, *Heave* and *The Memento*. *Heave* was a national bestseller, a finalist for the Amazon.ca First Novel Award, the Thomas H. Raddall Atlantic Fiction Award, and the Dartmouth Book Award, and was a *Globe and Mail* Top 100 Book. Her stories have appeared in numerous literary journals including *Best Canadian Stories* and have been longlisted for the Commonwealth Short Story Prize and the American Short Fiction Prize. She also co-created and hosted *Fear Itself*, a CBC national summer radio series. She holds degrees from the University of British Columbia, the University of Ottawa, and Acadia University. She was born and raised in Nova Scotia, where she still lives.

Instagram: @christy.ann.conlin
Website: christyannconlin.com

CHRYSTIA DONICA is the author of two children's books, *Kanne* and *The Champion*. *Kanne* is a national bestseller, a finalist for the Amazon.ca First Novel... and the Thomas H. Raddall Atlantic Fiction Award, and the *Chatelaine* Book of the Year, and was a CBC and *National Post* ... favourite. Her stories have appeared in literary fiction journals including *Grain*, *Prairie Fire* ... and *New England Review* and the *American Short Fiction*... blog. She also created and hosted her own five-part personal finance radio series. She holds degrees from the University of British Columbia, the University of Guelph, and Concordia University. She currently lives in Vancouver, where she still lives.

chrystaudonica.ca/blog
chrystaudonica.com